I BID YOU WELCOME

A collection of dark tales from writers in spirit

I0638813

Dorothy Davies

I BID YOU WELCOME

GRAVESTONE PRESS

AUTHOR'S INTRODUCTION

As a medium I am used to spirits walking in and working with me. There are a lot of books out there with my name on, all of which have been dictated by spirit authors. Richard Laymon arrived some time before we actually began work on the novel he wanted to write: he was just there, a companion whilst I fought my way through the process of getting the first channelled book into the public arena. Once the book was published, he began hinting that it would be rather fun to begin something which was not historical, which we did. We then started to write what felt like a non-stop stream of short stories which have been published in anthologies, both print and on-line. Richard asked me to collect them into a separate anthology as we worked.

In my computer the file was marked 'Richard's anthology', knowing that sooner or later the right title would appear. I thought for a while it would be When Our Graves Grow Cold, initially the first story in the collection (and my all time favourite) but it didn't happen because Bela Lugosi arrived to collaborate on the novel (which explained why it stalled for some weeks, the two men were in discussions) and I went looking at Bela's official website. His startling image and unmistakeable voice saying 'I bid you welcome...' was all I needed - we had at last pinned down a title.

Bela wrote stories with me, as did many others who walked in, smiling, offering their tales of death and destruction. Some only came once, having said what they wanted to say, others returned to give me more stories. My grateful thanks go to Roald Dahl, Edith Wharton, Charles L Grant, Virgil Grissom and Yul Brynner for their welcome contributions. Most of the collection was written by Richard Laymon, that I know. There was no mistaking the oft-times evil chuckle when he wrote something particularly gory...!

The invitation is sent out. Richard, Bela, all the other contributing writers and I bid you welcome to a set of stories that will, we trust, entertain and possibly chill you as you read late at night.

Enjoy.

Contents

7

Autumn Leaves by Edith Wharton
Road Rage by Richard Laymon
Burning Love by Richard Laymon
Countdown To Death by Antony Woodville
Life Changes by Richard Laymon
The Pied Piper's Story by Roald Dahl
Gabriel's Revenge by Gabriel
I Will Wait For You by Richard Laymon
Victims of War by Thomas Hartwell
Back Where I Belong by Richard Laymon
Blood On The Rose by Kathyrn Howard
Walk With Me A Way by Edith Wharton
The Perfect Crime by Roald Dahl
Santa's Special by Richard Laymon
Waiting For A White Knight by Richard Laymon
Endurance by Sir Ernest Shackleton
The Hunger Of The Moon by Virgil Grissom
The Day Death Wore Boots by Yul Brynner
For The Greater Good by Dorothy Davies
Now I Can See You by Richard Laymon
Will You Walk With Me A Way by Edith Wharton
Halloween Dream by Richard Laymon

I Bid You Welcome...

Bela Lugosi

The electronic butler stood by the doorway, nodding his head, bowing slightly to everyone as they arrived. 'I bid you welcome...I bid you welcome...' It was charming but monotonous. Angie, standing in her cloakroom cubicle ready to take hats and coats, thought if the thing said it one more time she would go mad, rush outside and rip its stupid head off.

'I bid you welcome...'

She gritted her teeth and pasted on the false airhead smile the company asked for.

'Well, at least you're real!' The comment from the suave silver haired man with the perfect smile was accompanied by what felt like a bank note. She bobbed a curtsy and gave him a genuine smile back. The coat was quality, the material as fine as any she had ever handled. Money, loads of it. And he was unaccompanied this night, too. Angie gazed at the man's retreating back, wondering how she could get to speak to him again. He had to come and reclaim his coat ... eventually ... could she hold out until then?

She looked down. It was a £20 note. She had never been given that much by anyone for such a trifling task as taking a coat. He had to be loaded. She had to speak to him again. This night. There had to be a way out of this dead-end job and into a life where money spoke and she need never want for anything again.

9

More guests, more coats, wraps, stoles, jackets, mink, ermine, silver fox, she knew her furs and she knew her 'customers.' Haughty to the very last, every one of them, hardly a smile, hardly an acknowledgement of her existence. Not like the silver haired man. He had noticed her, he had tipped her; he had smiled at her.

It was the only thing which kept her going through the long wearying end-of-year-party evening. That and the certainty that when she ushered the last guest off the doorstep and into a taxi, she could go out and get what she needed.

Blood.

The women acted as if she did not exist, except to hand back the fur, the silk, the velvet or whatever they had chosen to drape round their useless bodies that night. Not entirely useless, they were living containers for the elixir of life for some, but they didn't know that. Just as well, or they would not set foot outside their homes. If they knew the truth, they would hang a crucifix from every entry point, coat the windowpanes with garlic and generally act as if they were safe. They weren't. None of those things had ever stopped a blood sucking individual – and never would. No, they were not safe but the poor things didn't know that. Any more than they knew she had quietly noted down who they were and would look them up later – and perhaps pay them a visit. The thought made her smile.

'I bid you welcome...' She looked up, startled. It wasn't the automatic voice of the robot butler, but the silver haired man who was standing smiling at her. He leaned on the small counter which marked her domain from the rest of the club.

"Are you sick of the robot yet, my dear?"

"It's silent now but earlier I would have given much to have torn its head off."

She flushed bright red, wondering how she had the temerity to talk to a guest in that way. He saw it and laughed.

"Don't worry, I hate the stupid thing too and intend to ask the Club Secretary to do away with it. What's your name, by the way?"

"Angie, Sir."

"Nice name. I'm drawn to you, Angie, I'm not entirely sure why."

Angie didn't believe that for a minute. Men like this knew precisely what they were doing, who they wanted and why and then went and did something about it. This man wanted her and he was about to get his way. It wasn't for sex, she knew that, she wasn't pretty enough, well endowed enough or had overwhelming sex appeal. It had to be –

Could it be...?

"Are you not staying for the rest of the evening, Sir?"

"No. It's boring. I want – entertainment."

"I just want the evening to be over so I can go home."

"I don't think so, sweet Angie. I think you need the evening to be over so you can go out on the street – and feed."

"How did..."

"Takes one to know one."

She found his beautiful coat and handed it over with shaking hands, such was her excitement at finding another such as she; one who had

11

recognised her for what she was. Could she just let him walk out of her life?

Dare she just let him walk out of her life?

He stood, amused perhaps by her indecision. She felt the changes of expression chase across her face, saw his eyelids crinkle in anticipation of laughter – at her, or with her?

"I tire of the party this eve." He looked solemn then, as if awaiting her response. Angie's first reaction was that he sounded old fashioned for a moment. Her second reaction was, of course, he is as old as time – as I am.

"Is there no reason for you to stay, Sir?"

"None whatsoever. Nor for you, sweet Angie. Come walk with me."

It was not a request, it was an order she could not ignore and would not, either. She grabbed her own coat, a pathetic thing compared with the glories she had handled all that evening, and scurried out of her cubbyhole, the need, the desire, the thirst thronging through her veins. The fact she was walking away from her job and half a week's wages didn't matter in that moment. He offered her his arm and she took it, feeling the material flow under her fingertips. She felt shabby and yet expensively dressed at the same time.

Nothing was said between them. It was as if they had known each other for several lifetimes. They walked in unison; their thoughts seeming to flow in unison too. Her heels clicked on the wet pavements which were glistening with golden wealth under the street lights. She felt as if she could walk forever and never get tired.

He drew her to a stop on the steps of the parish church, looming, sheltering, impressively stone-like in the darkness.

"Tell me I did not choose badly this night, sweet Angie. Tell me you can walk into this building and come back out alive."

"But of course." She pushed at the huge ancient wooden door which, despite being locked, gave way under her touch and she walked in, defiant against the symbols of faith which comforted some and terrified others. The man followed her in and stood leaning against the font, watching her approach the altar without fear.

"It's fine, sweet Angie; it's fine. Now, come to me."

She turned and walked back to stand in front of him.

"I'm Constantine Williams. I'm the same as you. Countless hundreds of years old. For the entire time I have been Constantine I have not found anyone to walk with me, feed with me, share the eternal nightmare of being vampiric with me. Then I saw you standing there and I just *knew*. Will you share my life?"

"Willingly." She went into his arms as if she had never been anywhere else.

Later she would wonder why she was so trusting and then knew the answer, it was the loneliness. In every life she had taken on as a vampire there had been the intense loneliness until she had found someone 'like' to share her life with – for a while. It never lasted, vampire love never did. The driving need for blood set lover against lover, the demands

13

of eternal life meant that relationships palled, became violent, 'died' as only a vampire relationship could - in mutual acrimony with a good deal of hatred concealed and festering under the smiling skin.

But before then ... oh before then was the wealth, the sheer exhilaration of not having a worry in the world about spending money on anything she chose; the passion, they made love as if they were both going to die in the morning, day after day after day and it never grew any less, the conversations, ranging across hundreds of years and countless vampire lovers and never ever looking into the future, not for a moment, for to look forward was to cast a death knell over the love, the sex and the joy they were experiencing.

But everything changes, everything ends. Quiet words became nasty words, talks became arguments, passion became a torment of spite. Angie sat with a drink one evening, wondering where it had gone wrong and knowing that it had gone wrong this way many, many times before. It was part of vampire psychology, the need to be top, the need to dictate another's life and when that was two vampires together ... it went wrong.

There could be but one winner.

With a huge sigh she got up and went to collect a very large carving knife. The last row had been just that, the last one, in her considered opinion.

The electronic butler stood by the doorway, nodding his head, bowing slightly to everyone as they arrived. 'I bid you welcome...' 'I bid you welcome...' It was charming but monotonous.

Angie smiled at the butler as she went past. Monotonous it might be, but adorned with Constantine's perfectly preserved head, it was acceptable.

She wondered who she would welcome into her life that night.

'I bid you welcome...'

When Our Graves Grow Cold

Edith Wharton

When our graves are cold what do we do? What should we do? Lie still and shiver, causing the rotting flesh to fall even faster from our chilled bones or should we get up and dance around, get some friction going? Ah, but then the rotting flesh would fall even faster, tangle around our bony feet and trip us up. What a sight that would be! Part skeletons a-dancing around the graveyard, dropping gobbets of flesh everywhere, falling cranium over tibia and landing with an undignified thump on the newly turned earth. Well, you know that the earth takes a long time to settle itself after someone kicks it out of the earth's crust to make room for the coffin, then that person throws it all back in again in the hope it will level itself out after a few months. About the length of time it takes to install a lying gravestone, that is. Grass cutting is an ever-present need in a graveyard and graves that do not settle are liable to be skirted, leaving the swaying grass to nod toward the headstone and draw attention to the recent passing. Recent, that is, compared with the rest of them, the old ones, illegible through lichen and years of rain, snow, frost and neglect, through the slightly newer ones, not so much lichen, a little less rain, snow, frost but the same neglec ...

The thoughts are bitter this night. As bitter as the frost which cuts deep into the fleshless bones and chills the satin of the coffin. As bitter as the tears which fell when the coffin was interred and as bitter as the words which were uttered across the coffin from those who sought only that which was left behind. Inheritance. Death and inheritance. Linked forever in the minds of those who remain, those whose beds are not as cold as the graves in which we lie, face up, staring at the lid, wondering what to do with the idle hours.

We have gone. We have relinquished all control over tax matters, bank problems, fuel prices and everything else that plagues the world. And yes, those ancient gravestones indicate people who feel the same. Tax matters, bank problems and fuel prices have dogged the country for centuries. Fuel? Animal feed, the animals themselves, the cost of transport, the cost of stagecoaches, you name it we have endured it, now no more. It is as much a relief as the ability to dance with bony clattering over the cold graves, no need for clothes, no need for food or drink or medication. Freedom! Of a kind.

We have gone but we remain. A memory, a leaf on the family tree, a line on the order of service, a tear when a favourite hymn or song is sung - if we are fortunate. A fading figure in an old photograph. We have gone but, as with everything, a part remains. Even as the leaves fall and rot into the ground to provide sustenance for plants and the trees themselves, so we fell and our flesh rotted and went into the ground which enriches the growth in the graveyard, feeding the worms and burrowing things. They do not attack the bones. The bones are intact, left un-attacked, to dance around the stones which lie tip tumbled and faceless and wordless and sometimes lying and we would wish the truth had

17

been told about us. That we were bold and adventurous, that we were lovers and procreators, that we were movers and shakers – instead of husband, father, grandfather, whatever. We know that. We know what we were, the world knows what we were, the world doesn't know what we did whilst becoming husband, father, grandfather and all the other words inscribed at cost by the chiselling whistling stonemason at his bench, tap tapping away at the stone which would, in time, be defaced by lichens, rain, frost, snow and indifference.

When the flesh is gone, when the rotting is through and the bones are clean and sharp as new blades, ah, then we can rise up and dance.

We ask the most common question of all when we dance, bones clacking and resonating across the cold stone, what do living people think we do when we are in our coffins? Do they think we sleep, rest, think, feel, mourn?

The answer we give is that they do not think, because they do not want to think what we might be doing. Do not want to think that they might open their door one night after the sound of castanets is heard on the doorstep and find our grinning skeleton there, demanding entrance, do not want to think we have come to wreak vengeance for inheritances stolen, destroyed, unshared, do not want to think. We are dead. We are in our graves. There we are expected to stay, to be good corpses and allow the world to carry on its business without us.

But we get bored, us fleshless wind clad people. We get bored and restless and even if you had donated us a book or a paper, how long would that last in eternity?

And so we rise up with a clatter and shout of jubilation and dance the freedom dance across the unsettled graves, leaving footprints that are never seen, terrifying the wildlife that would otherwise venture into this memory laden cold portion of land, until those creatures run and the unsettled graves become more settled.

And when the dawn reaches out to tug away the curtain of darkness, we return to our narrow homes and stare once more at the coffin lids so that we do not upset those who might, just might, come visiting with flowers and tears.

And who go home to warm beds and warm homes and do not wonder what we do when our graves are cold.

One day they just might find out.

Do You Happen To Have...

Richard Laymon

Do you happen to have...

No, before I ask that question, let me explain why I need an answer. You know the best way to dispose of a body? Dump it in the cellar and let the rats feed. Simple, isn't it? How come no one seems to have done it? Oh, there's the small problem of what to do with the bones but – well, come night and a mallet, you can smash bones into tiny fragments which can then be tossed in with the household rubbish and who knows what goes into the back of the refuse lorry and then to the landfill site?

That's what I did with the charity worker who refused to accept 'no thank you' as a polite way of saying 'I don't care about your charity; I have enough to do catering for my own, thank you very much'. He would argue, so I invited him in. Fool that he was he came in, too, thinking he would convince me with his superlatives and his greased hair and his false teeth. He didn't, he just gave me a good deal more to smash up. Good job I don't have neighbours.

The rats fed well that night.

It's not that I enjoy killing, you understand. I am not that heartless. I just – like the power of life and death. I like to survey the person standing on my doorstep and decide whether they should live or die. Are they of any use to mankind; are they better off being disposed of? Those who come to deceive and steal, they are of no use to anyone so they become – well, rat food, basically. Other people go to the supermarkets and buy cat food and dog food; I get rat food delivered to the door. On foot. No effort involved.

The rats are multiplying, though and they need more food than they did when I began. Oh, when did I begin? Who was the first to meet his fate in my cellar? I think it was the simpering irritating canvasser for the local Tory party. I don't vote. Don't believe in it. Why waste time and effort putting a pencil cross – and how demeaning is that, I ask you? Make your mark, peasant! No signatures needed here! – to vote in someone who you will never hear from again. No, I refuse and I told this simpering twit I refuse.

'Suffragettes fought for your right to vote!' he insisted.

'No,' I said, 'you have it entirely wrong, little man. They fought for the right for women to vote. Not for me. I came into this world a long time after that right was given – and remember this, they didn't *win* the vote; it came about through the war.'

At this point he put a foot in the house as if to attack me, so great was his rage, so I stood back and let him in. Not a thought in my head at that moment of anything but – shall I be honest? Pure malice. I wanted to confound him; I wanted to flatten the ego with which he came. Instead I flattened his head and threw him down the steps... No I didn't, I rolled him down the steps into the cellar.

You see, I knew there were rats down there and I had done nothing about them. Animal lover, you understand, can't bear to kill anything. No traps or poison for me. So they lived there quite happily, cohabiting with me. I didn't bother them, they didn't bother me.

Until they got the taste for flesh.

It's a bit of a job keeping them supplied but I can do it, if I work hard enough at it. No sign on my door about 'no callers,' I welcome them.

Then I invite them in to talk. And tea. And a visit to the cellar – that's not optional, by the way, that's compulsory.

I started a new game last week. Not killing them first. Oh the fun I had hearing the squeals and shrieks and screams and hammering on the cellar door. They don't know I bribed the local builder to reinforce that door with steel. Looks like old battered wood on their side. What a joke, I laughed myself silly first time it happened.

I just have this small problem. The rats are multiplying and like I said, no traps or poisons for me, animal lover that I am.

There's only one solution and you might be able to help me with that.

Do you happen to have the mobile number for the Pied Piper?

The Fragrance of a Poisoned Flower

George Villiers, duke of Buckingham

You want beauty? I have it. You want wealth? I have it. You want flamboyance? Your current 'gays', if I may use that crude expression, have nothing on me! Sex? I could bed every last one of you and still look for more. But apart from that, the real thrill, the real reason for living, is power. And I have that, so much of it! Who else could work with and influence and dominate TWO kings?

Ask me if I love my wife. I answer, yes, I do, as much as I can love anyone outside of myself. Ask me if I love my children, yes, I do – don't ask me to repeat myself. Please. It bothers me to do that. It trivialises the questions.

Now ask me what really matters to you and what you, by 'you' I mean all those with questing grubby minds, of course, really want to know – did I bed King James.

No. He bedded me. End of discussion.

Well, of course it isn't, if anyone ever liked to boast of their conquests, it is me. I look in the mirror and see this handsome face looking back, oh the swirl of the moustaches, oh the set of the eyes, the curve of the lips, am I not the most favoured of men? Even now? Of course I am.

But then again, I have to say His Majesty was a most desirable man. I enjoyed his company, his wit, his intellect and his body - in no particular order. We were well matched, I have to say.

Does it matter to you? No, change the question, why does it matter to you? Why do I see comments such as 'this has caused much speculation' as if it is anything to do with any of you any way! In my time, that time of great mystery to you, being what you call bisexual was normal. We entertained men and women alike, why not? Why shut yourself off from all that walking talking enjoyment when all you need do is say 'are you willing?' or just crook an elegant little finger and the person comes running. I didn't expect the king to come running but close enough, close enough...

The way to win ultimate power is to be next to and in the confidence of the person with the ultimate power right there in his hands. Who better then than the king himself? So, you work at it, you make sure you are always there, always with the right smile, the right words, the helping hand, the comforting touch. Easily done, believe me, if you know what you're doing. That means never taking your mind from that which you want, power without the title that goes with it. If anything goes wrong, you stand back, it's nothing to do with you. Always someone else's fault. Every time. And every time it works, too. My wife exhorted me to keep right at the king's side from the start, she was right, too. Women often are; I have to admit this, even if I do not wish to admit it.

Power. Hint at something, get that something, wealth, property, estates, it was all there for the virtual asking. The trick was not to ask but hint in such a way you got it anyway. Then you could express great surprise and gratitude and hide the avaricious smile behind a look of intense love and affection. Not difficult to do, believe me. You are speaking with an expert; you understand that, do you not?

Ah, how I wish I were still on your side of life, there are so many of you who think you can do it and would benefit from just a little tuition from the master of the art. I am speaking to the men, you realise that, I trust. Women, in whatever shape or form they come, do this naturally. I wish I knew how. I became an expert through hard work; they are experts from the day they are born. I find this unfair but so far no one on my side of life has listened to my complaints on the subject. I wonder why?

Now you need to ask the next burning question, did I seduce the young Charles? Oh the books which have discussed this, oh the academics who have lost sleep over this! Fools, every last one of them, abject stupid fools. Books and academics alike.

I loved the young Charles; I never touched the young Charles. Do you know how hard it was to keep my hands off that slender beautiful body? But you see, if I had, he would have been useless to a woman and he needed to have a woman to produce heirs. James had already done that, he had already 'done his duty' to the country so he could do what he liked. When I knew Charles was no longer duke of York but Prince of Wales, he was off limits. Forever.

That would have been all right if it had not been for the meddlesome Henrietta Maria. In truth, I had to push her out of the way to write this, for she wanted to write this story and Heaven alone knows what slander she would have written about me!

But we had fun. Oh we had fun, we enjoyed ourselves so much, especially when we went to France and then on to Spain, supposedly in disguise but seriously, I ask you, how could someone such as myself not be recognised instantly? Of course I was and how I loved it...

Now I have told you all this, now I have spilled some of my innermost secrets, I come to the real reason for writing this tale of woe and unhappy spirit life.

You know, surely, I made some serious errors of judgement in France: of the 7000 men His Majesty Charles I entrusted me with, about 4000 were killed. Accidents happen, I told him when I returned, keeping quiet about the fact that I should have seen it coming and diverted it. And didn't. He said try again.

So we tried again. Those Hugenots needed help, I wanted to help, so I went to Portsmouth, oh invidious city! And began preparations for a new campaign.

And there, in that dirty place on a dirty dockyard, wearing my very best suit for the occasion, I was cut down, cut down I tell you! by a thoughtless sailor with no taste at all, believe me. No taste at all. Stabbed through the heart with –

It's hard to even say the words so they can be written, really it is.

A kitchen knife. A common or garden kitchen knife.

If you are to be assassinated how much nicer it would be to lie on the dirty dockside with a jewelled dagger standing proud of your chest, no?

And so, even to this day I haunt the realms looking for one John Felton, aggrieved sailor, man with no taste. I want to give him back his kitchen knife and hand him a decent dagger, one with at least semiprecious jewels in the hilt, and ask him to do the job in a decent manner. As it should be done. As it should have been done.

Perhaps then I will get some peace.

Danse Macabre

Edith Wharton

The silent figure on the gurney twitched, moved, sat up and looked around. The tag on her toe said JANE DOE which annoyed her very much. *I'm not a Jane Doe, I'm Lydia ... Lydia ...* The rest of her name escaped her, much as her memory seemed to have done.

Why am I on a gurney with a tag on my toe? Why am I cold and why do my veins look blue and stark and my flesh look like marble? I am NOT dead!

But – one chilled hand at her throat said otherwise. There was no pulse, no heartbeat, no warm blood rushing around a body that was beginning to sag. That annoyed her too. *My boobs never sagged! Now look...*

Look. She looked around, this dead Lydia, and saw she was in a morgue. A cold lonely desolate morgue that held no comforts for anyone, least of all those who were delivered there on a gurney and left overnight because the staff had gone home and not bothered with yet another stiff.

She swung her legs over the side and stood up. *Well, I can still do that. Now, can I walk?*

She could. Dead Lydia staggered across the room, round the dissecting table and got to the cabinets.

I need company! She pulled and tugged and reluctantly the first drawer slid open. The man inside, elderly, lined, haggard and half starved, blinked and looked up at her.

Is it time to get up?

If you want.

I do. It's boring lying here like that. Nothing to look at.

I need the company.

The man sat up and pushed himself off the tray which had been holding him.

That's a good idea. Let's find some more people.

With two of them tugging at the handles, the drawers came open a good deal easier. The young girl, anorexic and pathetic, clawed at their arms as they lifted her up. *Look at me, look at me, aren't I elegant and slim and beautiful?*

The truthful answer was no, but they did not say it. *You are, you are!* She beamed and spun round, her flimsy hospital gown billowing around her. *I can dance!*

We all can but right now we want company!

Lydia pulled at another drawer with the help of the old man and the anorexic. A dark handsome youth smiled with shockingly white teeth as he sat up. *Thank you! I thought I would be stuck in there forever!* One easy movement and he got up too, swaying to an unheard rhythm. *Is it time to dance?*

Let's get everyone out first. Lydia was in charge and didn't know how she had become in charge, it had just – happened. She liked it, though; she had never been in charge of anything. Always the underdog, always the low paid worker following orders. Now she was issuing orders and these people were obeying her. It was a miracle and she was not about to let go of the good feelings it was generating.

I'm naked! The shock ran through her but no one had said anything, no one had ogled her, no one had touched her. *Maybe, but it isn't right!* She went back to the gurney and took up the sheet lying there, wrapped it around her body and tucked the end in securely under one arm. That felt better.

Oh, elegant, the old man observed, without a trace of sarcasm. *You wear it well, dear lady. Swan-like, I would say. What's your name?*

Lydia.

Now if I remember my Greek mythology, there was a swan who went to Leda, which is close enough to your name, dear lady. I want to change that. You are a swan, wrapped in white as you are, as elegant as you are and as thoughtful as you are. Let's call you Leda instead of Lydia. It sounds so much more romantic.

Leda. Lydia. She turned the names over in her mind. *Leda will do fine*, she said eventually, with a big smile. *Thank you. No one has ever said anything that nice to me in my whole life.*

Well, they should have done. I mean, there you are, you had every chance to walk right out the door and leave, instead you opened drawers and let us out.

Well, it was because I wanted company, she confessed, rather than take credit for something that was not right.

He shook his head. *Maybe, maybe, but you had your chance and you chose to stay. Now, let's get everyone else out, shall we?*

Combined effort, they all worked at it, opening the drawers, releasing a white cheeked old lady with sharply knowing eyes and a loving smile, a middle-aged man still looking for his pens and papers, the reason for his existence, the little girl who had collided with a bus or a bus had collided with her, either way she was not pretty any more but no one said a word, they took her hands and they all danced round the dissecting table and laughed a great hollow laugh that no one else could hear but them.

The dark man told them jokes at which they all roared with laughter, the old lady told them of her children which brought tears to their eyes, the old man spoke of sunny days on a river bank fishing with grandchildren and some of them grew nostalgic. Then they danced again to refresh their senses and their spirits and their energies and told one another this was the best night they had ever had in their entire existence.

Dawn touched the sky with pink fingers. One by one, without saying a word why they were doing it, they climbed back into their drawers and one by one Leda, still in her white robe which made her look like a swan, closed the drawers with a supreme effort.

When they were all sleeping again, she gracefully danced a solitary dance around the room, remembering the feel of rhythm making the feet move, the thrill of a tune running through the head, the sway of arms and hands. Then she grew tired, it had been a long night and an exhausting one, but oh what fun she had experienced!

She climbed back onto the gurney, laid the sheet out and stared up at the ceiling, remembering how it felt to dance.

Just before she fell asleep forever, she wondered what the mortuary attendant would think when he found her tag on the floor.

Hairs On The Back Of The Neck

Richard Laymon

"It's not an unusual phobia, Mr Tomlinson. Many people are afraid of spiders." The hypnotherapist was calmness personified, as he should be, thought Harry. But he had no idea...

"It's not just spiders ... well, I suppose it is, really."

"We can treat this. Would you like to make an appointment? I'm sorry my receptionist isn't here today, if you could give her a call tomorrow ..."

"I will; thank you."

Harry put the phone down and cursed. Why couldn't he just tell the man the truth? No, it wasn't an unusual phobia but the situation he was in and that –

Could he just up and tell someone?

No.

"It's not like my house is dirty," he told his neighbour over the fence, a bit shamefaced but wanting to tell someone, "but I just found a jar of peanut butter in the fridge-"

"Not a good idea, Harry." Old Tam would interrupt, always had done. "It won't spread."

"I know, I went to put it in the cupboard and do you know? Its death date was two years ago!"

"Still be all right, though."

"Maybe, wasn't going to risk it, though."

"You had any more trouble with spiders, Harry? Remember one time when you said you had a giant one in there."

"Well, sometimes, comes and goes, you know."

"Don't like them much myself, but you know what they say, if you want to live and thrive – let a spider run alive."

"I do that, Tam, I do that. Can't bear to kill anything."

Especially the one I have in the house, he thought, but said nothing about it.

Someone else he couldn't tell.

"Is there anyone in the Pest Control department who knows about getting rid of spiders?" Next port of call, the local authority.

"Not really, sir, do you have much of a problem?"

"Well, there's one very large one..."

"We wouldn't send someone out for one, sir. Sorry."

But this one is ... no, they would call the people in white coats if he told them.

"Thanks anyway."

They'd be sorry one day that they didn't listen.

Harry went back into his lounge and stared at the spider which had all eight legs curled up under its huge body and took up the entire sofa.

"I just want my house back," he told it. "That's all. And no one wants to help me."

The spider reached out a long lazy leg and gently tickled the hairs on the back of Harry's neck.

"All right," he sighed. "You can stay."

Mother Misery

Richard Laymon

Now is it my fault Marty decided to disinter the corpse?

I suppose it's my fault I went along with it, but what do you do when your best mate says they want help to retrieve something of great value?

Well, you think, if he's that good a friend, he'll share the 'value' with you. Right?

So there we were, 11 o'clock on a night fit to freeze your hanging bits clean off, with specially dulled spades so the moonlight didn't shine on the blade – he thought of everything, did Marty – shovelling, or should that be spading? earth out of the grave of old Mother Misery. Now you should know that wasn't/isn't her name. She was actually Mrs Annabel Miller, but she was the picture of misery when she was alive and I didn't suppose she would be much better looking now she was dead and cosmeticked and combed and powdered and all the things that the undertakers do to make you look good. What for ... no, these were thoughts I could not speculate on as I sweated under my black waterproof with the effort of shifting the earth.

"What are we doing this for?" I muttered. Not a real question, you understand, just a – what are they called, reetoric or something, question. But Marty answered for all that.

"She was buried with a gold chain round her neck, see, and hanging from it is a pendant, see,

35

with markings on it which everyone says was the clue to her treasure, see, and I want it."

I gotta tell you, at this point I put down my spade and stared at my best friend who was still digging and sweating and I swear he was shit scared, so he was. I wanted to know why. I didn't want to ask why. I hoped he would tell me by himself.

He didn't.

So I had to ask.

"What's got you scared, then, Marty?"

"Me? Scared? Nah, you got it wrong, old mate. I just don't like digging up the dead, is all."

"So, why are you?"

"I'm not - we are. Get digging."

So I dug.

And the spades went *clang* on the coffin lid and we both jumped like someone had spooked us.

And the moon went behind a cloud at that very moment and we were in total darkness. I swear Marty squeaked like a mouse but I can't prove it and would never mention it to him anyway.

Now I'm not saying I was the big bold friend who never got scared, 'cos that wouldn't be true but I swear I wasn't as scared as him. I did hope he didn't notice the strange smell coming from my pants.

He carried right on working, I give him that. Scraping the earth off the coffin lid and making enough space for him to get down there and start unscrewing the lid. Well, he was no bigger than a whisper, so it was easy for him. I'm a bit – bigger than that.

The screws came out easy but then, who would have thought, when they put them in, someone would be along to get them out again? He tugged and pulled and then, there she was, Mother Misery, in all her rotting glory.

And there was the gold chain in all its shining glory, like it had just been cleaned.

And do you know he lifted that chain off over her head so delicate like I was shocked and moved. I truly was.

Before you could say Mother Misery no more than ten times, the lid was back on, the screws in place, Marty was out of the grave and we were demonically shovelling the earth back in. The moon came out again to help; I just hoped Marty thought the damp patch he could possibly see was a night shadow. Then I realised first, he had the self same damp patch and second, I could smell the same smell from his pants as from mine and knew he would not dare say a word.

"Let's get outta here!"

I never heard more welcome words from anyone. We legged it out of that cemetery like we were training for the Olympics. At the street corner he banged my shoulder with his fist.

"See you tomorrow, mate, thanks for that." And he was gone, racing for his home like demons were after him. God, I thought we got out of the boneyard fast enough but the speed he went was amazing.

I slunk indoors, ripped off the soiled pants, bundled them up and put them in a carrier bag to put in the rubbish, washed myself off and crawled into bed. And spent the night remembering the look on the old girl's face when the lid came off.

She looked as if she was gloating.

Anyway, Marty come round the next night and we went down the pub for a pint or three and he pulled the chain and pendant out under cover of the dark corner we were in and showed it to me.

There were the markings all right, but hell, they could have been anything. Would have needed someone with specialist knowledge to decipher them. Marty said, "got to go see a witch tomorrow, someone what knows about these things. She said she can read the signs."

"How much?"

"Doesn't matter, when we find the treasure..."

Now comes the strange bit which I can tell you worried me more than a little.

Marty started losing weight. Like, loads of it. Like, he were no more than a whisper before, then he was all ghost. No body at all to speak of. No voice, he just about gave out a hiss. Had no money, spent it all on finding a witch who could read the signs and lead him to the treasure. Not a one of them could do it.

Marty stopped eating last week. They said it wouldn't be long before he was in his grave. He said he couldn't eat, it was choking him. He said he wished he'd never gotten hold of the damn chain and pendant. He offered it to me and I refused it. He said I was sensible and he wished he'd refused it.

I went to his funeral today. Would you believe that he was the next person to die after old Mother Misery, so he's buried right alongside her?

No wonder she was gloating. All she has to do is reach out through her box and he's right there, isn't he? The man who stole her pendant.

God alone knows what she'll do to him.

The Blood Makes Me Whole

Richard Laymon

Did not ask come. Did not want come. Do not like here. Do not like people. Do not like planet. Air heavy -- make sick. Ship damaged. Cannot go home. No ship come for me. Need own food. Food here make sick. Do not like language. Words hurt. Need something stop words come me.

Universe endless. Home many times away, many, many times away. Home pretty colour, pretty sound, no words.

Two legs found me. Two legs frightened me. Two legs say I very big, I scare, I frighten, but two legs not run. Look with orbs in head speak with slit in head. Sound comes from slit hurt. Two legs not know I scared of two legs. I want stop two legs speaking. I afraid what I do so do nothing.

I take from head of two legs words to say what I do, why I here, I do not know all words; I do not know who two legs is. More come look at me with orbs in head and speak to selves point speak I not speak back. Not know how speak back. Not possible.

Stand. All two legs run and stop. All two legs look me shake like ship when it damage.

More two legs. Come with strange feeling, feeling hurt. Two legs not afraid me. Two legs go in ship and stay long time. I do not like two legs in ship. I go in ship. I see two legs look at my ship. I know they not know what is. I know they not mend ship. I know I not leave planet. I hate planet. I take feeling from two legs and know feeling right.

I hate.

I take one two legs and drink lifeblood from it.

I feel good.

I take more lifeblood.

I feel good.

I grow.

I leave ship and all two legs make loud noises run from me.

I think -- new for me -- they try kill me.

I take from their heads. They not understand.

I am now whole.

I feel sorry for two legs; they not know they cannot kill me.

I can kill them.

I understand.

I can stay here now.

I can feed.

The blood makes me whole.

The Kingmaker is Dead, Long Live The King

Richard Neville, Earl of Warwick

Welcome, friend. I see you start; my apologies, I have frightened you. It is so rare I find anyone who is capable of hearing me so when one such as you happens to arrive, I forget and rush forward to talk, for the loneliness becomes unbearable at times. It is I, Richard Earl of Warwick, who is speaking with you at this time. I believe you know me if only by reputation, I who once owned half of England, I once employed 30,000 people in my estates, all there to serve me - and my wife and my children and those I took under my wing.

Have you visited Warwick Castle? If you have, can you tell me how it fares? It is some time since I have been able to go there. I would wish for a chance to walk the halls and corridors again, to sit by the hearth in the great Hall, to have a wolfhound at my feet and a goblet of ale in my hand and stories of victorious battles in my mouth. I would wish for these things, but I am bound here, the place I fell, the place I died. For one such as I, this is not a good way to pass eternity.

What does the name of Barnet to mean to you, I ask? Do you know of the battle which took my life, do you know of the background, how I came to be there?

I am rushing you with my questions and I needs must stand back for a moment for the colour has lost your face and left you as pale as the wisps of mist that haunted the battlefield that night, the night before Barnet, the night before -- as I understand it -- orders were disobeyed and the Yorkist men cut me down. I understand that even at the last the King was mindful to be lenient. Thinking on this, as I have these hundreds of years, I believe it best that I died, for I would not wish to have been beholden to one I once held in my power. It is not possible to have been one of the greatest men in England and to the content that the King that I put in place should grant clemency to me. I was the kingmaker. I was a supreme ruler.

And now? What am I now? A restless footloose fretting lonely revenant tied irrevocably to a piece of land on which my human form gushed blood and whose life force became what you now see.

***

Kingmaker! Who does Warwick think he is? Does he wear a crown? Did he fight old Henry's forces and win; did the triple suns shine on his battlefield? Did he ride in triumph to Westminster to be anointed and ordained King of England? I think not! More than that, did he ride through Micklegate and see his father's and brother's heads impaled on spikes? Again, I think not. If he had, then God's teeth, he would have been as filled with anger as I was – and am. I have not released it; I will not release it until all Lancastrians are dead or have sworn fealty to the House of York! Do not the shades of my revered father and much loved brother haunt me even now? Do they not stand in attendance at every meal when I sit at the table and walk with me to my chamber at night? Do they not ride alongside me, harness jingling, hooves clattering, words silently issuing from long stilled mouths when I go out to see my people? My uncle is alongside them, but it is my closest relatives who make themselves known to me and I can tell none of their presence, not even my brother of Gloucester nor my friend Hastings, those who usually share my deepest thoughts. This is my burden, my destiny, my ambition and one I will fulfil, no matter who is killed along the way.

Warwick was good for me. I confess that to the darkness of my room, to the hangings which shroud my bed, to the pillow which cushions my very thoughts. My cousin was good for me. He taught me much, especially how to stand up to the world and be the man the world expects to see. His advice was good; be larger than you are in every way and you will become larger than you are, in every way. I used his influence, his many associates, his reputation, all this I freely confess, but in turn it was freely given. I thought long that he was no more than a loyal relative; never giving thought to the fact he might believe he was controlling me. Me! Edward Earl of March, King of England, the fourth such to hold that title! Warwick, controlling me! It is an outrage, it is beyond belief.

So, do I confess now that my marriage to a Lancastrian widow – fertile or not – was a direct blow to his hold on me, or do I admit that I fell in lust with the outstanding beauty of the woman and the fact her womb was proven to be fit for child bearing and thus give this country the heirs it needed... or do I admit it was part and part...

Whoever you are who is standing by to hear these confidences, hold them close to your chest as you would your coins in a high stakes game of Tables, for these words are not for the world to know. Let them think on that their king is a man of firm decision, not swayed by a pretty face and even prettier bosom. Ha! Edward, you fool yourself if you think they think otherwise, for your philandering is widely known and smirked about, with envy, I might add, with distinct envy.

Warwick, cousin of mine, stay your hand, there is no need for us to fight. My rule, my country, my throne, my crown, my decision. Grant me your fealty and let us be done with the fighting.

***

He was mine, a puppet king, guided and pushed by my guidance. He called himself Edward IV, but in truth he was no more than the right arm of myself, Richard, Earl of Warwick. He would argue otherwise, he thought himself to be a free thinking man making his own decisions, choosing his own wife and oh, did ever that burn deep in my heart!

The night we camped beyond Barnet, myself and my men, loyal, indentured, committed to the Warwick cause. That night the moon was an enemy, the orders were not to allow its rays to glint on sword and halberd, on battleaxe, pike and lance. That night there were wisps of mist about, they seemed unreal, they seemed intent on distracting the men. On that night before battle, they seemed to come with malicious intent and I was almost afeared. Such wisps take on the form of night maidens, come to steal the substance of men, to take subsidence from them, to weaken them before the battle on the morrow.

It was that I feared more than the maidens themselves. If ever a leader needed his men to be strong, it was I that night. I could say nothing to my advisers or my squires, for they would have thought me weak and that I could not tolerate. My burning wish was to walk outside my tent, my shelter, to move away from the men and the women who follow them, and commune with my God for a while. Instead I had to stay there and show leadership, confidence, smile brightly, tell them we would overcome the Yorkist forces next day. I did not add, for it was unnecessary, that the future of the house of Warwick depended on them. Would they have cared? Ah, that was a foolish question I asked myself, for their livelihood depended on the house of Warwick standing at the end of the battle. And how could the house of Warwick stand if its head was not in place? And so they were honour bound to ensure that I lived, even if it was to fight another day.

I ask even now where did it go wrong with my puppet king? I had it all worked out. First make a big fuss of the boys, Edward, Richard, George, seek their loyalty and allegiance in all things. For a time it worked, but then just as I planned the new King's future, an alliance with a European princess to create a dynasty, the fool produced a commoner, a Lancastrian wife, fertile, two brats clinging to her skirts and I had no doubt another waiting to be produced. I knew well of Edward's proclivities, anything female that walked. And what did this marriage do for the house of York? It divided it, for George Duke of Clarence was immediately disinherited from the succession. And did he not brood on this, did he not come to his cousin, did he not ask for ways in which he could take the Crown?

I could have sworn that one of those wisps was beyond the door flap of the tent, listening intently to everything I was thinking, ready to report back to the others. I was not a superstitious man but that night appeared to be laden with dark deeds, with sorcery, with evil doings and I was unsettled in my heart and mind.

**

What of capture and power, what of my dallying when the rallying cry when out that my brother of Clarence and my cousin of Warwick were staging an uprising? There is much I could talk of and think of at this time: exile and the loneliness of Europe after the court of London, the malevolence of that witch Margaret of Anjou, the treachery of my own brother whom I loved – but not as much as I loved my brother of Gloucester, I do admit. Mayhap he knew it. In truth, when I married the woman I fell for, I disthought of my brother being disinherited of his claim to the throne. Oh I knew well that Clarence meant heir, in dynastic terms but it became a name, no more than that, and I thought nothing of it until Hastings, in one of his rare moments of lucidity, pointed it out to me. Then I realised what I had created, a viper in our hearth. My stupidity in denying my brother of Clarence the woman he wanted, the Kingmaker's daughter, for no reason other than spite, I do confess, and so he went ahead and married her anyway, in Calais and I was not invited, though many were.

My problem was, I scarce thought ahead on personal things, whilst busy planning ahead for things which concerned my country, and so I ignored the fact that a wife brings a family with her and ere long the court was overrun with Woodvilles, all seeking titles, honours and marriage partners. Oh, and a sharp faced all knowing, all seeing mother who stopped at nothing to promote her family's interests. I blame her not, the Yorks had long since done the same.

So let me, for the moment, go quietly by the politics and go to the heart of it, Warwick captured me. His king. Held me prisoner in his castle. Refused me access to my lawyers and family, strutted around like a proud peacock crowing his victory over his king. And Clarence, smiling and strutting alongside him, thinking he had the very crown on his head already, before a declaration could be made. Fools that they were, how could they have thought it would last?

Gloucester arrived, with Hastings and a crowd of men at arms and I walked out and bestraddled a horse and rode back to London, with a huge smile and a sense of rightness. It was their turn to flee.

Little did I know that Warwick was turning to the Lancastrians for succour and support. Had I but known that, he would not have lived a day after I walked out, cousin or no. Sometimes the knowledge you need evades you. It did that day. Long did I regret it.

***

He had the luck of the Devil or the Devil on his side, I knew not which it was, nor did I question it at the time but since I have long pondered on this. I had him in my power. For a long and exhilarating time I had the ultimate power, the king of England in captivity. And yet he walked free. It was as if we were spellbound, enchanted, I cannot think how or why but the men arrived, Gloucester and Hastings at their head, the doors opened and he walked free. Clarence and I stood there and let him go.

Now, whatever you may think, you who are listening to this confessional at this time, it makes little to no sense for a person holding a king in his power to let him walk and then ride free. Am I not right on this? So what enchantment was cast that it be so? I looked for cause and ability and found it in the mother of his queen, the thrice damned woman who had caught the king's attention and foiled my dynastic plans, made me look foolish in the eyes of Europe. What dark spell did that accursed woman cast? There were rumours aplenty about her witchcraft, nothing substantial, nothing on which to base a trial but it was there. And it was there I sought my answers – and found none.

The wisps of mist outside were laughing, silently but they were laughing. I knew then that the battle would not go my way. Knew it as any soldier knows that the weather is changing and not for the good of his side of the fight to come. Knew it in the bones which ached in the dampness of the evening and the night, even as the night stars peeked at times from cloud which threatened rain but never delivered, just played with the moon enough to annoy those trying to shield themselves from the enemy.

Enemy. Men I knew, men I walked and broke fast with, the king, his brothers, for by then Clarence had left me and returned to the Yorks, on his knees in the dust begging forgiveness and it being granted to him.

Again I ask, what possessed the man I thought of as my puppet? Anyone who takes up arms against the king, no matter their kinship, is a traitor. But he forgave him, embraced him, took him back into the house of York and let him ride out with him against me, the kingmaker, at Barnet.

Clarence, and the men he promised to bring to my cause – to put a Lancastrian king back on the throne.

What foolishness possessed me that I would think it would work?

***

No one knows of this but in exile, as we talked away the long empty days and drank away the long empty nights, I consulted an alchemist. I wanted my crown back, I wanted to sit on the throne of England again, pass judgment on those who offended, praise and honour those who did not. Grant a good living to the peasantry and the minions who served the court. Honour the Woodville who fled into exile with me, Antony Woodville, the best of them - apart from my wife. He was patient beyond duty with Gloucester, who was surly at being in Europe when he wished not to be, with Hastings who I knew well he hated – and knew too that the feeling was mutual – and with his king, whom he honoured at all times.

I consulted a man recommended to me by the wench who served me in her own way during my exile. A man needs a woman. I say no more on that. She knew of this alchemist who dealt with the dark forces and so I went and I saw and I discovered and I knew I had found the right person to get me back to England and where I wanted to be. For the gold I borrowed and the gold I promised he raised a daemon who he said would walk with me at all times.

I feared it. I knew it was there when I sensed its presence and smelled the rank breath it had, not sulphur and fire but dead things long rotted and yet not returned to the earth, unholy things, those of the Devil himself. But I was grateful for it, without such a backing who can walk back into their country, displace the king and place the crown on your own head, retrieve your wife from exile and announce to the world that you are back in control? Not without more luck than any living man is entitled to.

But oh I feared it. For it was a fickle being and could turn on the one who mastered it without a moment's hesitation. And, I ask myself, did I master it or did it consent to work for me for a while, before returning to its supreme master? I know not and I dared not ask.

I tell you this, unseen person listening beyond the hangings of my bed, I paid the gold as promised, even though it was difficult to find the right honest person to convey it to Europe without stealing a single part of it.

From the moment the daemon cast his lot with mine, money was found for ships, horses and men, not to mention arms and supplies.

It withdrew its support almost immediately, for the weather turned and we were laid up in port for some days. Then, when we sailed and I thought all was well, a storm that must have come from Hell itself reared up and destroyed a ship with all the men and horses on board and scattered the rest of our small fleet along the coast of England. No matter, we were home and all who were important – forgive me, those who perished in the waves – were safe. Gloucester, Hastings, all of us gathered together to start our march to London.

And this time the daemon was in a good mood for by trickery, we invaded York and the men of York changed allegiance and marched forth with us.

And my brother of Clarence changed allegiance and came to meet us and ask for forgiveness. The daemon said I should, so I did. I wondered if any other noted the darkness which sat on my right shoulder and breathed its rotten foulness into my nostrils. They wondered why I granted forgiveness to a traitor. My master, the daemon and he who controlled the daemon, told me to. And that is the truth, may God be my witness.

***

By what trickery did Edward get back to England in storms and high seas, by what trickery did he confuse and baffle the men of York and persuade them to march with him? What turned Clarence ... I could go on. I will not go on.

Battle was set; we were to meet at Barnet.

I had to set my mind to think this was not my cousin, not the boy I had seen grow up into a giant of a man who terrified all who saw him on the battlefield, sword besmeared in gore and innards, his armour besplattered with it and his face afired with blood lust and battle fever. A man who courted women with a smile and a kiss and bedded them instantly. A man I admired and loved and wished he were my son, for all I loved my daughters.

I heard talk that he was not the same man who fled into exile, that this time he came as a conquering king, he came with dark forces behind him, for how else did he survive a winter storm so hard none could remember one such like it? How else did he gather to himself a growing army of men ready to lay down their lives for him?

Such talk was dangerous to the morale of those I had with me and there was nothing I could do to buttress their feelings against it. Dark forces scared the wits out of the simple soldiers, who saw nothing wrong in fighting their fellow man if bounty were at the end of it and who, if I were honest, had little else to live for in the lives we had then but who could not fight the unknown, the daemons of hell.

The wisps came closer and gathered together. They became a thick mist. I knew then that the battle was in danger, for men who cannot see kill the wrong men and cause havoc and confusion and end up fleeing.

And thus it was.

In the very early hours the Yorkist army moved against ours in a thick white mist that obscured the outlines of the forces, so that it was difficult for those fighting to see where the armies began and ended. They clashed hard and long, the cries of the wounded almost drowned the noise of weapons on weapons and on helmets and armour. The screams of the horses were worse.

I heard the cry of 'treason!' go up but realised in the mist, demonic as it was, for sure it was no normal mist, such was its thickness and blanketing density, that the men were firing arrows at their own.

Some were running, then more and I thought I had to leave if I was to live and fight another day.

They came for me out of the mist, men with blood lust and battle fever writ clear on their visages and I had no chance and no choice. I was pulled from my horse and slaughtered.

Here. Where you stand right now.

And even as I lay there, with the death rattle in my throat, I heard my king yelling 'Bastards! I said let him live!' and knew that at the last my kinsman had been merciful. On that thought I died.

***

He lay dead, my cousin, my kinsman, my mentor and my friend. He lay dead and the mist curled around him as if in comfort, as if to blanket him. And I yelled my frustration and anger and grief at those who disobeyed my direct order to let him live.

The daemon whispered to me, *what would you have done with him?* And I had no answer for that. All I knew was - I did not want him dead.

Your price for winning the battle was the death of him for whom you cared.

Then I understood.

I stood tall among the carnage and watched as the mist lifted, swirled and went away. I knew I was truly King then, with none to challenge me. Oh, there was one more battle to come but the Lancastrians were weakened with the loss of this once great man and the battle was in my hand before we even fought it.

Gloucester came to me, blood streaked and weary, Clarence right behind him. We stood and looked down at the corpse of him we had loved. I smelled the foulness of the daemon and wondered if it would now leave me, for its task was done.

As one the three of us clasped mailed fists above the fallen kingmaker.

The daemon whispered *the kingmaker is dead, long live the king* and in that moment it was gone.

With it went my peace of mind, for I knew this great man's death was on my conscience and his blood was on my hands.

I had to live with that for the rest of my life.

***

Welcome, friend. I see you start; my apologies, I have frightened you. It is so rare I find anyone who is capable of hearing me so when one such as you arrives, I forget and rush forward to speak for the loneliness becomes unbearable at times. It is I,

Richard Earl of Warwick, who is speaking with you at this time. I believe you know me if only by reputation, I who once owned half of England, I once employed 30,000 people in my estates, all there to serve me - and my wife and my children and those I took under my wing.

Have you visited Warwick Castle? If you have, can you tell me how it fares? It is some time since I have been able to go there. I would wish for a chance to walk the halls and corridors again, to sit by the hearth in the great Hall, to have a wolfhound at my feet and a goblet of ale in my hand and stories of victorious battles in my mouth. I would wish for these things, but I am bound here, the place I fell, the place I died. For one such as I, this is not a good way to pass eternity.

What does the name of Barnet to mean to you, I ask? Do you know of the battle which took my life, do you know of the background, how I came to be there?

Let me tell you my story and then I have a request for you. If you would be so kind.

I wish to beg whatever daemon controlled my young cousin at that time to come and rescue me from this hell. I cannot face spending the rest of eternity trying to find someone to speak with me about my time, to keep my memory alive. Oh I know he was daemon led, no man could do so much and survive, such luck is not for the taking, not for the likes of mere mortals.

If you visit Warwick Castle and find him there, the King I mean, I beg you to ask him to do this one thing for his cousin, find the daemon and beg him to release me.

Would you do that for me?

Richard Neville, 16th Earl of Warwick, says 95% of this story is based on fact; the rest is embellished to create a tale worth reading. He asks you to consider the incredible luck of Edward IV and ask yourself whether he had daemonic help or not...

A Lonely Place

Richard Laymon

This story was inspired by a quote we found:
'Even when you're dead you shouldn't lie down
and let yourself be buried.'
Gordon Lee.

It's an odd fact that the morgue can be a lonely place at times. I mean, empty lonely, desperate empty, that kind of lonely. Don't quite know why that should be, it's just a place like anywhere else. Ain't it? Well yes, I mean I know there's bodies there, course I do. They don't do no harm just lying in their separate drawers, each one with a name on the front that sometimes matches the name on the tag, if the police done their job proper and got the right people down to say, "yes, that's him" or her, or sometimes, it, if they didn't like the person. Happens, you know. Trust me, being there when it happened. Knows all about it, I do.

You know you thinks I ain't all there and you might be right but then again I knows things that you don't. Like I knows what happens when them that don't like the dead one comes in. Ah they pretends a bit at first, "oh how sad it is, oh what a shame" and stuff like that. They signs the papers, they go outside and they say to one another "well that's it done and dusted. Now I guess we have to bury it."

See, I been there, I hear them, I see them, I know.

I likes wandering around here in the dark, suits me nice, this does. No one to bother me, no one to tell me to get out, no one to say "you ain't supposed to be here, get yourself out." Cos you see, they don't like coming here after dark. They think them bodies is gonna get up and move about and cause a few problems. Like that's gonna happen. Them bodies is shut away in them drawers and they ain't getting out to someone opens it. And who's gonna open them drawers this time of night?

Pretty damn silly if you ask me. Was you asking me? Well, I done told you anyway. So now you knows whether you wanted it or not.

I likes it in here 'cos it's warm and safe and I ain't gonna be attacked like I would if I was out on the streets. Makes no difference to them what's out there that I ain't got no money or stuff on me they might want. No, stuff they do want. So I creeps in here and I stays here all night walking about, thinking about them bodies in them drawers, wondering if I open one, would someone get out and talk with me a while, just give me sommat else to think about in the long night of dark and empty and desperate when I think I would give just about anything to talk to a human being.

I'm trading safe and warm for lonely. Well, tis better than having my head bashed in and ending up in one of they drawers with a made up name on the tag which don't match the one on the front, seeing as no one around here knows who I am. So, right glad I am you dropped by tonight so we could have a talk.

Well, I thought we would talk but here is me blathering on and you saying nowt. Come on, you must have sommat to contribute. Right?

Thought so. You're scared, you're one of them that shouldn't be here 'cos you don't like it. So tell me this, how come you're here? How come you got through that fire door that I know well I jammed it solid so no one could get in? Oh I undo it before I go, wouldn't be fair to the staff to be trapped in here with a fire, now would it? It's just that when I'm here at night I like the door locked proper; then I know I'm safe. I mean, what if one of them out there saw me come in and thought it would be a lark to follow me in?

You gonna talk to me or what?

Looks to me like it's 'or what,' not a word gone past your lips.

Here, is you real? Or is you one of those ghost people what I do hear about and never did believe in? Prove it to me, shake hands.

Well now, would you be looking at that? Went right through me, that did, that hand of yours about a substantial as a smoker's breath on the last drag of a ciggie. Right then, which of them drawers is you? Oh, that one. Interesting. Not sure if I should tell you, all right I will. You was one of them where they said 'it'. Didn't they like you? You look so sad, tells me they didn't. Hold on a minute, you was that suicide, wasn't you, the one what threw himself off the bridge? Well now, if I had relatives like that, think I'd have done the same thing. Don't blame you in the least.

Listen, it's getting on for dawn. One or other of us had best be gone, better still, both of us better be gone before the staff arrives.

Which way you going? I mean is you gonna leave here or is you gonna hang around with your body? Ain't a lot of good to you, is it?

Wanna come with me? I got this nice place under the bridge, got me a little den there, brew up some coffee and if I'm lucky a bit of toast in front of me fire. You're welcome to share. Serious I am, we can share, because you don't seem to realise we're both on the same side of life, mate. Just 'cos your hand went through mine didn't mean I'm alive and you're not. Your hand went through mine 'cos I'm a ghost, too. Ha! Your face! You thought I was a human and could see a ghost, right? Well, I like to play that trick on people, works every time. And you fell for it!

This morgue can be a bit of a lonely place at times, see, you need a funny trick or two to pass the time. It's been a few years since I had someone to talk to.

Right glad I am to meet you.

Coming?

No Witnesses

Richard Laymon

The building was long, sleek, silent and black. Workers went in, workers came out. Faceless people, formless uniforms, silenced by some decree or other, for they said nothing of what they did, what they saw, what they earned. They came, they went, mysterious as the phases of the moon to those who did not understand.

The regulars in the Vic Tavern were intrigued. They spent hours over pints of dark ale discussing what could possibly go on in there, who owned the place, who benefited from the 'production', if there was any, why the workers weren't local people who were starved of work.

Niall Jones, landlord and resident seer, swiped at the bar with a fresh cloth. "I say it's government, always did, always will."

"You can't be sure, Niall, you can't be sure of anything in that place." The objection came from Will Hamilton, the oldest of the group and a habitual drunk. He clung to the edge of the bar as he would a lifebelt; the floor had stopped him many times on his way down. He did not want to repeat the performance as it brought nothing but derision from his mates.

The youngest of the group, the dark haired, ever smiling dare devil Shane McBride, slapped a note on the bar top.

"Anyone wanna bet I can't get in there and find out once and for all?"

Niall eyed the £20 and grinned. "I ain't a betting man, Shane, but these others..."

Money piled up on the bar. Niall picked it up and put it in one of the tankards hanging overhead. "There 'tis and there it'll stay till you come back with proof, young Shane."

"What sort of proof?"

"Sommat they're making in there, course!" Tom Hartman smiled over his beer. "You do what you said you'd do and you get the cash. Damn it all, I'll double what's there if you do it!"

"Done!" Shane got up, drained his beer and then shrugged his shabby leather coat round his shoulders. "I'll be back when I've got the proof. Thanks for your belief in me, mates!"

Outside in the cold night, Shane put the jacket on properly and pulled the collar up to protect his neck. With determined steps, he headed in the general direction of the black building. It had been dominating the local countryside for some time, everyone knew where it was, no one knew what it was there for. Now a bet had been laid in his favourite pub, Shane was determined to find out. He knew there were security guards; he also guessed that sometimes they were rather lax, because no one ventured near the place. Its very blackness and bleakness put them off. Or so the talk went, anyway.

Up close the building was even more ominous in its appearance than he thought possible. The walls, sheer black as they were, seemed to invite graffiti and yet there was not a single mark on them. There was no sign to say what company the building housed, no entrance or exit signs, no car parking signs either. Did everyone know which way they had to go, where they had to park? Were the workforce that organised, that disciplined, that they needed no signs? It added to the mystery of the place, which may or may not have been intentional.

Light shone in a very narrow band down the side of a side door. Shane edged close to it and listened. Nothing. No hum of machinery, no sound of feet. He found his stomach churning and wondered whether he had drunk too much beer, or whether his nerves really were getting the better of him.

Nothing ventured, nothing gained. Clichés sometimes helped, but on this occasion they didn't. Still he stood there, hesitating. The truth was, he was flat out scared and didn't mind admitting it – to himself.

It took a supreme effort but in the end he pushed against the door and it swung open. Inside was a huge cavernous space criss-crossed with beams and suspended from the beams were –

Bodies.

Hanging by the neck, swinging slowly in the draught created by the open door.

One swung round to face Shane, its mouth cracked apart in a rictus grin that scared him more than the sight of all the 'corpses.' He began to back away but was stopped by the door slamming shut behind him. He thought he would drop dead with shock when a hand landed on his shoulder.

"Who do we have here then?"

He could not turn round, could not face whoever it was who had stopped him running for his life, although a tiny part of his mind said 'it's the security guard, fool!'

"Do you have a voice, stranger?"

The grip left his shoulder and Shane slowly, reluctantly, turned and looked at the man. If he was a security man, it was one strange outfit he was wearing, metallic one piece suit and helmet that all but covered his face. His hands were encased in metallic gauntlets and he wore heavy boots of matching material. The effect was startling - and scary.

"S... sorry. We had this bet, see..."

"That you could get in here and find out what we did. Right?"

Shane nodded dumbly. Put like that it sounded pathetic.

The man laughed; a very unpleasant sound. "Been a few of those over the years. That's why we leave the door open. We know you're all bursting with curiosity; it's better a few come in and find out the truth than the whole population descending on us one night with torches and pitchforks. Oh, been there a few times, my friend, more than a few times. Right, you want to know what we do? We make drones."

"Drones." Shane knew he sounded stupid by repeating the man's words but he was lost for anything sensible to say. Who needed drones?

"These aren't bodies; they're drones in the making. They're drying off before being fitted with their equipment. Gave you a bit of a turn, though, didn't they?"

Shane nodded. It was safer than trying to speak.

"Is that enough for you?"

"No, to win the bet I need to take back proof of what you do." The words came out in such a rush it was a wonder the man understood them but he did, for the coarse almost angry laughter sounded again.

"And you want to win the bet, right?"

"Well..."

"It's not the money, is it? It's your standing in whatever club or pub set up the bet."

At that moment the nearest drone body swung round and an arm brushed Shane's head. He shrieked and ducked away. "It's alive!"

"No. Nothing's alive here but you and me, friend. They're empty. The filled ones are in the next room. Do you want to see them?"

Shane had the distinct feeling he had no choice. The man was already stalking through the hanging bodies, pushing them away as he went. Shane hurried after him, but not close enough. The bodies swung back and collided with him as he passed. By the time he reached the next room he was nearly out of his mind with fear. No matter what the man said, the grinning faces had nearly been the cause of releasing his sphincter muscle.

The door was opened and the metallic man gestured for Shane to walk in.

Then the true horror of the place struck him.

The drones were standing in rows, reminding him of the photos of the terracotta army he had seen, only in this instance there were endless lines of identical beings, all pointing machine guns at him. The faces were ferocious, implacable, stony, each with its rictus grin, horrifying in their obvious need for –

Blood?

Where had THAT thought come from?

"I like you." The voice was almost as metallic as the outfit. "You have guts. You didn't run. Others did. Now, how can we prove to your friends what we do here?"

Shane had gathered his senses – just – and was beginning to accept that the drones were models, not real men. They were obviously for some film set somewhere. The company was obviously involved in very special effects of some kind. It was obviously...

And there the thoughts ran out of steam. What if he was wrong?

"What? Er ... I mean ... well ... I ought to take one of these – drones with me to show them."

"Ha! If we do that, my friend, it would mean we could leave no witnesses."

Befuddled, Shane tried to work out what he meant. He tried again. "We could just take one, couldn't we?"

The man sighed. "Yes, we could just take one. It would walk at my command and we could go to this pub of yours. But – we must leave no witnesses. This place is top secret. Are you prepared for that?"

Shane was confused, scared; boosted by the man's compliment that he had guts... his mind spun in all directions, none of which made sense. Of course there would be no witnesses; it was only his mates, after all.

"OK."

"Then let's go." The man released one of the menacing drones from the 'army' and did something to it. The drone began marching toward the door. Shane got out of its way, the thing was

67

unstoppable, it would have walked through – or over – him without knowing he was there. For the first time the fear he felt on entering the building seemed no more than a passing summer chill, this was all out fear verging on terror. What in the name of heaven had he started? And could he stop it?

"Listen..." he began, but the man waved a metallic fist in his direction.

"You asked, you get." The mouth clamped shut behind the helmet; there would be no more words.

Shane ran after the drone which was heading for the Vic Tavern as if programmed to go there. He tried getting hold of its arm but he was no more than an annoying fly. The drone kept right on marching. The man in his metallic suit, even more frightening in some ways, marched right after it, almost keeping pace with his creation.

They reached the pub and the drone smashed open the door. Shane saw everyone leap to their feet in shock. The drone stood still, as if awaiting further orders. The man in his metallic outfit stood, arms akimbo, feet straddled, in the centre of the saloon.

"This here person..." he pointed a thumb toward Shane, "wanted proof he had breached our security and found out what we do. Well, here it is, men. We are making drones – to take over the world. Unfortunately your friend overlooked the fact that I clearly said we must leave no witnesses."

As the words were spoken, the machine gun burst into action and everyone in the room was mown down before they could utter a single cry. Niall slipped down behind the bar, leaving a smear of blood on the bar.

The drone turned its rictus grin to Shane who backed off, hands held up, shouting "No, no!"

The metallic man had the same kind of meaningless grin under his helmet.

"No witnesses, friend. I did say."

The machine gun fired one last time and Shane crumpled to the ground, a riddled corpse.

The metallic man tapped the drone on the shoulder. "About turn! Quick march!"

They returned to the black, long, sleek, silent building and the drone went back into line.

At daybreak workers went in as usual. Faceless people, formless uniforms, silenced by some decree or other, for they said nothing of what they did, what they saw, what they earned. They came; they went, mysterious as the phases of the moon to those who did not understand.

There were no witnesses. There never would be.

The Tourist

Edith Wharton

He was just like any other mark, you know? Scruffy sort of guy, tweed jacket, slacks with not much of a crease, bit of a stubble thing going on. Balding a bit but who isn't? Big nose, I remember the big nose. Washed out sort of eyes, not much colour there. Looked like he hadn't got two pound coins to rub together, if I were truthful with you.

He gets in the cab at Liverpool Street Station, wants a trip round London.

OK, I says, let's go! Where do you wanna start, sir?

He says, that thing near the river, that tall thing you see from the sky.

I says, do you mean the Monument?

He says, I do that.

So we goes to the Monument. I sits in the cab while he climbs the 300 odd steps to the top, I sees him go round the viewing platform, I wait while he climbs back down the 300 odd steps and I think, rather him than me. I'd rather sit here in comfort, off me feet, watching the meter tick on. This is the good one; I remember thinking, the rare good one. The one we all talk about getting and few of us do. Go round London seeing all the sights. Usually from the windows, mind you, this one was different, getting out to see places, leaving the meter running.

Oh be sure I kept the meter running. I might have had Princess Diana in my cab and I would have kept the meter running. Fat chance of that, before or now. Oh but I loved that woman... Enough! Just gotta say no one would have made me drive that fast and kill the one true beauty who walked our planet. Oh hell, here I go again...

Forget it. Let's get back to the weird one.

I've been driving a cab in London all my working life, me. Love it, I do, all the people, the sights you see out the window along the streets, them's as wanna talk to you about London and all it has to offer, them as hates it, only here on business or 'cos they gotta be.

Not this mark, though, he was - different.

He wanted the Tower next, so we went to the Tower. And I sat outside and waited while he did the tour round, seeing those – what do you call them, the ones in the outfits? Can't remember. Anyway, he went there.

He wanted the London Eye after that, wanted to see, what was that strange new building called? Can't remember. Well, we went there.

He wanted Buckingham Palace, wanted to see the – damn it, where's my memory gone! The men in red outfits and tall hats? Well, we went there.

And we went on like that. All day we went round and round London and all day ... I just realised ... my memory got worse and worse till I could hardly remember how to get from one place to the other. Like I was in a fog, you know?

And come to think on it, he got –

Smarter and smarter as the day went on, clothes got better, he got more hair, he got less beard. His eyes got more colour. And I got – older.

And I forgot things. It was like – he was some kind of vampire and he was draining me of all my knowledge.

Next thing I know he's driving the cab and I'm in the back, watching the world go by, wondering where the hell I am.

We went back to the Monument and I got out and he drove off. I opened the door and climbed up the 300 odd steps to the top and when I got there, I thought, how odd, he said 'the thing you can see from the sky.' How did he see it from the sky, I asked myself. And I asked myself who he was to drain me like that.

And I found myself on the viewing platform of the Monument and everyone who came up walked right through me and I knew I wasn't human any more.

Then I realised he wasn't human either or he wouldn't have been able to take over like that and put me in the back of my own cab and then drive off in it and I'm lost, lost, lost and only you've seen me in the last ten years.

I'm right bored with the view, but that ain't the real problem.

It gets damn lonely up here, I can tell you.

Transformation

Bela Lugosi

The invitation was a whisker short of tacky, black Gothic type face, blood dripping from the capital letters, the whole bit. Grant looked at it and was tempted to throw it in the fire but then put it on the mantelpiece instead. A vampire themed party. It might just be fun. A chance to get into the suit, find the fake blood, slick back the hair and make himself look like Bela Lugosi – he bore a startling resemblance to the old horror movie star if he dressed properly and flattened his normally abundant hair.

If the invitation had been a little bit classier, he would have been just that little bit more enthusiastic about going. But then, the Palmerstons had never been class, they were aspiring snobs, the sort of people who tried really hard but never quite got it right. Full marks for trying but ... they never would make it. They hadn't grasped the concept yet of not trying, that class came naturally.

Grant had a week to prepare himself for the party. Having decided to go, he got a haircut, to make it easier to emulate the great Lugosi, got the suit dry cleaned, told them it was for a wedding, hung up the cloak and brushed it daily to make sure all creases were out of it and polished his shoes several times. They had to gleam. They had to reflect – well, he would work on that when he got there.

Against all expectations he felt a frisson of excitement at the thought of partying once again. He hadn't been out socially for a long time. As he was both single and no longer young, he tended to be overlooked for parties; he had his uses as a fill in for dinners when another male was required to balance the table and where he found himself chatting endlessly to society 'girls' who only sought a husband. Grant was not husband material. He knew that and held on to it, too. He had long since decided that his lifestyle did not permit him to share it with another.

Something about the time and place of this invitation made it a little more special, too. First it was on Friday 13th, auspicious for such an occasion and second it was in an area of London he didn't know. *A different hunting ground.* Now where had that thought come from, he asked himself, as he stared into the mirror whilst he shaved.

Whatever, he was, for the first time in ages, aware of a tingling through his veins and a need to be out there socialising again. It had been too long.

***

The party had just about got under way when he arrived in a part of Kensington that was both exclusive and yet shabby. Shabby-rich, he told himself as the taxi drew up outside the house. It was almost 'we have money but we would rather spend it on fun than on property.' Interesting - and that was before he got a foot in the door.

He leaned through the open window to pay the driver, handing over a £20 note and magnanimously waving away the change.

"Thanks, Mr Lugosi!" The taxi driver was obviously a fan. Grant grinned, showing his fangs and watched as the man smiled in obvious appreciation. "Love the outfit!" The taxi drove away, leaving Grant on the pavement, staring into the distance, breathing in the exhaust fumes and wondering why he didn't feel sick from doing so.

The steps to the front door had been coated in 'blood', setting the mood before he even got through the front door. That was not blood marked, but scored deeply, as if by monster claws. Nice touch, he thought. He went to ring the bell but the door opened and a statuesque blonde stood there, wearing a skin-tight basque, thigh high boots, fishnet stockings and a flowing cape. Her makeup was way too heavy, she could barely see through the mascara mask and her lips struggled with the weight of blood red lipstick.

"Hell-oooo." The word breathed out in admiration. "And I thought I looked good!"

Grant held out his hand. "I'm-"

"Bela Lugosi, of course. I am so pleased you could make it tonight, sir." She stood back and let him enter the house. So be it, thought Grant, she's the second person in less than five minutes to see the great man in me, so I will be him for the evening.

The large room was hung with black curtains, slashed here and there by a 'knife' with 'blood' trickling down to pool on small tables round the black candles. The lights were dimmed and the music, heavy satanic rock, was way too loud. A typical party, he thought, every effort made and then made again so the effect was overkill rather than just kill. No subtlety, he thought, but that had disappeared a long time ago. About the time Mr Lugosi was making his terrible B movies, in fact. The room was jammed solid with 'vampires', all wearing the obligatory cloak and false fangs. The smoke from many cigarettes and the incense burning in holders around the walls made it stifling. He wondered how long he could stand being there.

"Bela?" Someone was calling. He turned to find the source and saw a small man completely dwarfed by his heavy cloak gesturing to him. He pushed his way through the partygoers, some of whom stood back and smiled and muttered his name as he passed them.

"Bela, I am so pleased you could make it tonight." The man held out his hand, which was cold, wrinkled and repulsive. Grant shook it carefully, then let go, surreptitiously wiping his palm under his cloak.

"How could I refuse such an invitation?"

"Well, you know the Palmerstons, obviously, or you wouldn't be here, but – I didn't think you'd come to one of their vamp bashes."

"It's been a while since I ventured out, thought it might be fun."

"Good, good." The man eyed him with a strong element of curiosity. "Forgive me, but you are Bela Lugosi, aren't you?"

Grant had decided to play the game, so said nonchalantly, "but of course."

"How did the Palmerstons get to meet you, I wonder?"

"Why shouldn't they?"

"They're not that high up the social ladder, if you get my meaning."

Grant moved aside to let a caped butler go by with a tray of drinks. He snatched at one, spilling the red liquor over his hand. Damned if he was going to stand there and chit-chat without a drink of some kind. The noise level appeared to go up a few decibels and he had to talk loudly to make himself heard.

"I've only met them once or twice, at other parties. I was surprised they had my address."

The man chortled. "So am I! Which cemetery is it you live in these days?"

Grant smiled. "Known to only a few, friend, only a few."

A woman standing by turned round and stared. "Mr Lugosi! How good to see you!"

Grant bowed in what he thought was a most elegant way and it seemed to impress, for the woman's eyes flickered in admiration. They were not as heavily made up as the vamp who had opened the door to him, she could at least see where she was walking.

"Are you here for the entertainment?"

He frowned. "Nothing was said about entertainment. I thought this was just a party."

"Oh, all parties need entertainment these days, none of this 'standing around chatting to all and sundry' evenings any more. But then, it's been a while since you were in social gatherings, isn't it?"

77

"It is indeed." Grant bowed again, not as deeply this time, just enough to acknowledge the truth of her words.

Others had turned and were advancing on him, hands outstretched; calling for 'Bela' or 'Mr Lugosi' and Grant was beginning to wonder what was going on. He didn't think the likeness was that good, but...

"Ladies and gentlemen!"

Everyone turned to stare toward the source – Geoffrey Palmerston, in a flamboyant red lined cape, was standing on a small stage in front of the black curtains.

"I am so pleased you all came tonight. I hope you have enjoyed the drinks and food provided. Now it's time for our entertainment."

Grant looked at the glass he held, wondering how he had managed to drink it without realising he had done so, unless he had poured it on the floor during his theatrical bows. He might have done. He certainly hadn't seen any food passing by on trays or any other way. Well...

"Mr Lugosi, I am so grateful you honoured us with your presence tonight." Geoffrey was waving to him. "Please come up onto the stage and let us all greet you properly."

It wasn't supposed to go this far, thought Grant, but what the hell ... he pushed his way through the gathering, realising people were beginning to stand back and let him pass them by, and got up onto the stage. The applause was thunderous.

Geoffrey looked flustered and pleased. "Good to see you, sir." He shook hands with Grant and looked at him with a fan's adoring face. "I never thought I would ever get the chance to meet my hero."

"Well, I'm here now."

"Your English has improved no end," quipped Geoffrey, looking at his guests, who dutifully laughed.

"I have been here long enough now to learn the language." Grant had a reply ready before Geoffrey had finished speaking. The guests laughed even louder, why, he had no idea.

A chair was brought out, a gilt throne-like chair with red upholstery. "Do take a seat, sir, and have a first-hand view of our entertainment."

"Thank you." Grant sat down, allowing his purple lined cape to fall open and his glittering shoes to reflect the overhead lights. He bared his fangs again and noticed one or two women step back. Yes, he thought, be scared! Unlike everyone else here, mine are real!

The curtains were drawn back with a clatter of rings and a sigh from the guests. Bound to an inverted cross in the middle of the stage was the statuesque blonde who had opened the door, now divested of her clothes and her makeup. She looked surprisingly young and innocent – and worried.

"My dear," Geoffrey exuded fatherly concern and consideration. "Are you ready to be our entertainment for the night?"

"Don't have much choice, trussed up like this," she smiled, but still with the slightly worried look.

"You volunteered, my dear..."

"I know. Let's get on with it, shall we? This isn't much fun, hanging upside down."

Grant pretended total nonchalance, as if this entertainment was something he saw every night of his life. It wasn't difficult, in his dreams he did. He just wished he could understand why he felt as if his bones were lengthening and his spine was straightening, why he felt as if he was not himself. And why had no one, not one single person, including his host, referred to him as Grant? Did he really look so much like the dead silent movie star?

Was he turning into the dead silent movie star?

Geoffrey turned to him.

"Would you like first bite, Mr. Lugosi?"

"Thank you, but no." Even the voice was changing, it now sounded so much more like the great man than it had. "Let everyone else have their chance."

"Very gracious of you, sir, I have to say. Ladies and gentlemen... your entertainment awaits you."

There was no movement at first and then the whole crowd seemed to rush forward, to climb onto the stage, to attack the girl. Blood flowed freely as they tore at her limbs. One man crawled on hands and knees to reach her throat which he ripped open with one bite.

Grant stood up, pushed the chair back and left the stage. No one noticed him leave.

No, not Grant - Bela.

He was walking differently, he was taller, the cloak no longer trailed at his ankles. He made it to the hall and glanced in the mirror as he passed. There was nothing there.

"We need to leave." The voice was silent, only in his ear. He nodded and hurried down the steps. It had begun to rain; the 'blood' on the steps was running into the street.

"Taxi!"

By a miracle one was cruising past. It pulled over to the kerb and Grant/Bela got in. "Evening, Mr. Lugosi, where can I take you?"

Grant/Bela managed to say his address and sank back in the seat. What the hell had that all been about? What about that girl? Surely she was dead! Did they think that was entertainment? Why –

He ran out of thoughts. Something terrible had gone on there, mass hysteria, perhaps, mass murder, perhaps, for surely they would have turned on each other when she was dead, if they had killed her.

"Here you are, Mr Lugosi. A pleasure to be of service to you, sir."

"Thank you." Another £20 note disappeared. Grant watched as the taxi drove away before wrapping the cloak around his body and walking down the road, toward the cemetery.

Vampires. The Palmerstons and all their guests had no idea. None at all. You didn't rip someone to pieces in the name of blood and entertainment, you find someone, you take some blood, you let them live a little longer so you can take some more and then some more. Only then do you take them into the world of the undead and only if they want to. Otherwise you let them go, to regret for the rest of their days that they never took the chance when they had it.

Grant became aware a figure was walking alongside him, a taller more upright figure than he was.

"I am you and you are me now." The voice was indisputably that of the famous star. "You are a true vampire, my friend. You understand it well. You have kept yourself clean of infected blood, of unwarranted attention, of the claws of women. That I admire. From now on, you and I will be one. Are you ready for that?"

Grant smiled. "I am."

"Then come with me, and we will become one. And then we will go and feed."

Snow Dancer

Edith Wharton

Snowflakes dance, don't they, as they spiral down from the thick rich darkness of the clouds, pirouetting and sashaying and even tango-ing with the others as they fall. Blown here and there by the thermals, they create a magical image before sliding into the white death that is their fate, stacked one atop the other on any available surface, no matter how slender, there to rot until the time comes when they melt away, their final ending, returning to the matter from which they came.

The man rested his large forehead against the cold pane, staring out at the whiteness. He had heard you could go snowblind if you stared too long but what did he have to see if he lived, anyway? Nothing but the unheeding world, the bustling people who had no time for a man alone.

What was wrong with being alone? Why did everyone have to have a partner of some kind? 'Not even a pet?' Eyebrows were raised as the question was asked. Who needed a pet? Who needed the sycophantic love of a dog, the arrogant independence of a cat, the silent needs of a goldfish when there were –

Ah, when there were places to go and people to see beyond the imagination of those who questioned his living alone.

He turned from ever changing display of snow dancers and looked around his room. The piles of newspapers were threatening to topple; if they did, they would resemble a snow scene like the one outside, albeit one speckled with soot. Or ink. Or dirt. Living alone, he thought, meant he could do just that, stack up the newspapers, ignore the dirt and stand and look at the snowscape for hours if he wanted to without someone nagging him to clear this, eat that, take a walk, take a bath...

Did the newspapers rustle? Did the dust on the table lift and fall? Had she at last come in from the cold to be with him? He could see nothing, no hint of movement, no sense of another presence. How long did he have to wait before his love returned to him? Had she not promised, with her last breath, had she not said in that gentle way of hers, 'believe - I will be back.'

Was the problem that he did not believe strongly enough?

He looked for her every spring when the new grass thrust its way through the unremitting coldness of the earth chilled by the winter winds, in the summer amidst the brightness of the flowers and the bustling busyness of the animal world going about its on-going need to ensure the survival of the species, in the autumn, waiting for someone to disturb the leaves that covered his lawns and still they lay, still in silent glory. How many years now? Five, ten, how long could he stay watching, waiting, whilst his mind narrowed to nothing more than the need to see her again? From time to time he would ask himself how long the money would hold out; then he would dismiss the thought. When it happened, someone would tell him, they would hammer on the door; say they had come to reclaim the place from him. Then they would look around and see the towering piles of papers and the dirt and the dust and they would put their hands over their noses because of the smell, the smell of things rotting.

Sometimes he thought he should remove the corpses, bury them beneath the lawn, but if he did that he would have to disturb the leaves which had fallen in such an artistic way, or he would have to disturb the fresh fallen snow and that would not do either, for had she not said, 'I love the way nature arranges itself.' Her wishes could not be undone.

He turned back to the window to see that the snow had stopped falling quite so heavily, the individual flakes could be seen, dancing for his eyes alone before becoming trapped in the white death.

One of the corpses was hers. In what moment of madness had he struck down, in what second of insanity had he snatched up the iron and crashed it into the side of her head? What had she said that had so enraged him? Long gone. Long, long gone. Did she forgive him in her dying moments? Did she say 'believe – I will be back' because she loved him or 'believe – I will be back' because she sought revenge? Sometimes he thought one thing, sometimes he thought the other. Either way he welcomed and feared her return.

And the other corpses? Those who had come looking for her.

He could not understand why no one had actually tracked down the fact that his home had been the last call for the people who came and never left. Perhaps it was because they were not 'authority' and perhaps because he had no neighbours. The only living beings who would have seen relatives come looking were the birds, the fox, maybe the badger who snuffled and slunk his way around the garden at night, half seen in the moonlight and ignored. Just as the visitors were ignored, until they became persistent and then they were added to the corpse room. With the door shut the smell was not too bad. After a while you didn't even notice it any more.

The snow had stopped falling. Silent white world, nothing moving.

Nothing but the snow slowly lifting, lifting, lifting and transforming itself in a shape, a familiar shape, a once loved shape, one that was walking soft and cold over the packed snow and not leaving a single impression as it passed and as it passed the cold blankness on the front of the head changed and moved and became the once loved face and then, for the first time, he was truly afraid.

He had no choice. It came closer and closer, it pointed to the front door. As if motivated by something he could not understand or resist, he negotiated the piles of papers, knocking some of them over into the ink stained snowscape he had imagined and went to open the door.

She stood there, smiling, totally completely white and frozen.

He stepped out to meet her, against his will, against his entire logical mind. He had no choice. 'Believe – I am back.' Did she speak, did she project, did he form the words in his own mind? Before he could decide the door slammed against the side of the house and the snow, precariously perched on the slates, cascaded over him as she caught him in her snowy arms.

Together they went down into the white death.

87

When Wightlink Became Darklink

Richard Laymon

I came off the ferry with great hopes, glad to be back, happy to see my island again. I vaguely wondered who was in the car in front of me and who in the car behind, were they as pleased to be on the island as I was?

My rear view mirror showed a hint of darkness and then it was gone. A passing cloud, perhaps, I thought, pushing the speed from dead slow to slow to faster and then finally meeting the legal speed limit. I wanted to get home.

There it was again. A hint of darkness. What was it? The day was brilliantly bright and sunny, the sky as blue as I had ever seen it, that clear polished blue that the island seems to boast most of the time, at least in memory anyway. The truth is probably we have more than our share of rain, being subtropical, but thinking about my time here I only remember the sunshine.

So where... and why... the darkness?

It was not a very long drive from the ferry terminal to the car park where I was authorised to leave my vehicle. I took my bag from the boot, locked the car and set off for home.

I felt as if someone was walking with me. I turned quickly but there was no one there. Yet I am sure I heard footsteps, the susurration of clothes, a hint of indrawn breath, as if I were sitting to fast a pace for someone.

But I was alone.

I stood in the middle of a mostly empty very large car park, which I had to cross to reach my street. I turned 360° but I was completely alone.

At least, that is what I told myself, but when I made my turn was there not that hint of darkness spied from the corner of my eye, my peripheral vision picking up what the clear vision could not see?

I hurried on, my heels clicking on the surface which changed from Tarmac to concrete as I walked across the road and found the pavement. It was foolish to tell myself I felt threatened, I was safe in my own narrow residential street, I was within five minutes of my house, the keys to the front door were my hand and yet a pulsing terror consumed me.

I increased my pace, despite the fact the road sloped upwards, making it difficult to walk fast and not breathe heavily. So close, I was so close, I could see the entrance, I hurried, I fought for breath, battling the terror as much as the physical effort of walking so fast.

Inside the gate, the latch dropped into place, the bolt shot, I finally felt my heart beat returning to a semblance of normality. I looked all round the garden, I was alone.

What in the name of heaven had travelled from the ferry with me? What had invaded the island, courtesy of my car?

I put the key in the door and turned it -- and walked into the darkness which awaited me.

(Wightlink is the name of one of the Isle of Wight ferry companies which plies its trade between Portsmouth/Lymington and the Isle of Wight. The other company, Red Funnel, has a name that would not have worked so well...)

Towton Nightmare

Antony Woodville

The array went out, once more we were to take up arms against the king – and if you ask which one, then I say the question is a fair one. There can be but one king to rule a country, all else is not fair and right in the sight of God.

I am Antony Wydeville, eldest son of Richard Wydeville and Jacquetta, Dowager Duchess of Bedford. I was a Lancastrian because the Wydevilles were Lancastrian. My father served the late Duke of Bedford, a Lancastrian duke and was held in high regard by His Grace King Henry VI, for all that he was unsound of mind and frail of body. Ah, but the she-cat who called herself his wife, Margaret of Anjou, ruled for him and so our queen is Lancastrian. What more did an aristocrat need to make up his mind where his loyalties lie?

The array had gone out, for once again the pretender to the throne, Edward Earl of March, son of the late Richard of York, former heir apparent to the throne of England, called himself King and wished to settle the matter once and for all.

So we rode out yet again. My mother clung to us in turn, begging us not to be in the thick of the fighting, to stand back from the crush if we could, to come back for she could not live without us. I would wish even now that I believed her, but it was not the entire truth. My mother could live without any of her children but my mother could not live without my father. He was her life, her love and her soul. Should he be killed, she would cease to exist as a person.

And I noted well that she clung to him twice as long as to me. I was not hurt by this, I understood my mother only too well, knew of the great love they shared. We had left for battle before – and returned. There was always the possibility it would not happen this time.

Our men at arms, equipped and outfitted at our cost, stood around the courtyard waiting patiently for us to mount up and ride out. They too had been through emotional farewells with their family. I knew not what thoughts troubled their minds that cold March day as we faced the journey to Towton, I could not begin to penetrate their minds. I knew only that my insides were jelly and if I did not hold tight to the reins and lean against my courser, I would fain have fallen with the fear which gripped me. I wondered if my father felt the same way.

Finally he put Mother from him and, with the lightest of kisses, mounted up and turned his back resolutely. I followed him out of the gate, my squire riding a little way back from me. I heard the tramp of feet and rattle of arms as the men followed, the supply cart trundling along behind them.

How difficult it was to ride away from a home where nothing but love was felt, where security and safety were taken for granted, to ride away wondering if you would ever see it again. Suddenly that which was familiar became beloved, as if your heart would break if you really believed you would not ride back through the ancient gate and into the courtyard, that stable hands would not rush to take the reins and lead your horse away and leave you to walk into the house, to be met by faces you knew and trusted, to be given food and ale that was good...

I urged my horse forward a little to ride alongside Father. His face was set in stone, I knew not what he thought or felt, whether his fear was as deep as mine, whether he believed he would return to his wife and his many children, whether he would share his thoughts and let me know I was no less a man for being so terrified.

He did not. We rode on all day and he said not one word to me.

He spoke eventually, when we camped, to ask if I had troubled bowels – indicating fear. I said I did and he smiled. "I too, my son, think nothing of it. No man who rides to battle goes without fear in his heart."

I wished long he had told me earlier in the day, I would not have felt so foolish or useless, but perhaps – if I were being kind – he had his own demons to slay before he could speak. I took the words for what they were, true wisdom forged on the battlefield for my father had fought many engagements and survived them all.

So far whispered my own demons. That I knew and knew well, there was always a last time. The great duke of York fought many battles but Wakefield was his last. My sister's poor husband, Lord Grey, ended his life at St Albans. What sorrows do we put ourselves through for the sake of a king...

And told myself that was treason and I had best think Lancastrian and be ready to fight the damned

93

Yorkists to maintain a Lancastrian king on the throne of England.

The trouble was that the demon that whispered to me asked if it was worth the sacrifice, as if which king we had made any difference to our lives, in truth and in reality.

I forced it back into its box, wherever it had come from for yes, it did matter. Mother was the queen's favourite, she had the queen's ear; she had the ability to ask for favours – and got them. Who knew what would happen with a Yorkist king... but to think of defeat was not a good way to direct the thoughts. Victory had to be for the Lancastrians, no matter what.

The weather was foul, bitter cold and rain which felt like ice. Our water was frozen come the morning; we had to break the ice to drink. Only partially fortified, we marched on.

Palm Sunday.

The day our Lord rode into Jerusalem on a donkey, with the crowds yelling 'hosannah in the highest' and other such utterings, if the priests be believed. Seems to me that the sun must have been shining that day for there is no sign in the Good Book that He was wearing a cloak, no, in truth, they threw their cloaks in the road for Him to ride over!

So why then had Heaven turned its face from us this day and given us the greyest of skies and the coldest of winds and the bitterest of enemies awaiting us on the other side of this bedevilled field of death?

I care not what people say to me when speaking of this battle and that, of conflict overseas, of fighting the Moors and others that are passing strange to us, there is no battle, no conflict that equals the bitterness of Englishman against Englishman, there for no other reason than booty after the fighting is done. Why else would they walk away from home, wife, family, to risk all on a battlefield if not for the loot they could bring home from the dead bodies of their fellow countrymen? What thought did they contain in their minds that they might be the fallen and their bodies the ones to be looted and thrown into a common grave?

'Tis evil personified, a battle such as this, Lancastrian against York, for nothing more than the glory of their Lord and master, he who owns their pitiful dwellings and grants them the right to farm a little land and take the bounty of the lady of the house at festival times. Ah, I speak with bitterness this day but this day is bitter cold, a cold to bite to the very bones that support the armour and help me sit astride this fighting animal whilst those who labour on my estates trudge through the cold and the mud and the dung dropped by the horses walking ahead of us.

I have been dwelling on one sort of evil personified. Why should Englishman fight Englishman? Tis well known His Majesty is catatonic more times than not and, disregarding the she-cat of a Queen who fights his battles for him, it is surely no more than a matter of time before he goes to his eternal rest and then, of a surety, Edward Plantagenet can make his claim for the throne again. He is popular enough with many to ensure he gains the vote, but I think on this in vain, for Edward is a soldier King and will fight for that which he believes to be his.

What evil is abroad in this country that we commit ourselves to one battle after another? It is as though power carries its own destiny, for many that is to find themselves just another body in some godforsaken part of England in an unmarked grave.

I allowed these thoughts to consume me as our leaders conferred and began the placement of the troops, the better to ward off attacks from the Yorkists. Many of our side had only come from York, were fit and strong and not in the least afraid of the young king's men, who had come a fair distance and would be weary before they began. I wondered how they could be so valiant. My body was fit to betray me, I was eaten up with fear now that the time had come to flight.

I stayed close to my father, hoping we would be placed together, and we were.

Everything seemed to be going well – until the snow came. We were already cold, chilled to our bones and our armour feeling like ice if we touched it, our weapons sheer blocks of ice too. The snow added to the misery of the day.

"Fear not the cold!" Somerset shouted. "Soon we will be knee deep in Yorkist corpses; they will warm us with their blood!"

Cheers and hollers greeted this sally but I detected with some despair that it was not as full of enthusiasm as I would have expected. But then, my experience was limited. I was, on that day, only 19 years of age. One year older than Edward's brother, Edmund, Earl of Rutland, who died at Wakefield on the battlefield, murdered, it is said, in cold blood rather than fighting. I did not wish to end my life that way. If I had to die this Palm Sunday, I wished to die fighting the hated Yorkists. But in truth I wished to live for there was much I had not done and still wished to do.

We were scarce in our place when the Yorkists arrived, lining up before us, shouting insults, shaking their weapons, trying to be fearsome. Our answer was a shower of arrows – which I realised were falling short because of the fierce wind blowing in our direction. We had faces full of snow. I began to feel a cold worm of fear which was stronger than that I had felt all through the march and the wait and the placement. The Yorkists had more on their side than we bargained for. They had less men than us, they were more tired than us but the wind blew from them. They held their fire, they watched the useless arrows fall and then began their own rain of death, snatching up our arrows and using them against us. The screams, the cries, the howling wind combined to create a sound unlike anything I had ever experienced. I was frozen to the spot until I saw the Yorkist men follow through their bombardment and charge toward us.

I know not if anyone fully understands the term 'battle fever' or if they believe in it. It exists. It is a blind red rage that takes away all fear, all hesitation, it makes you scream obscenities and charge at the man in front of you, whoever he might be, aiming to smash his face and head in with a battle axe, or thrust a sword into the weak point of his chain mail or cut his arm or leg so that he cannot fight or run any more, to force him face down into the mud so he is trampled and suffocates and saves you the task

97

of actually killing him. In the name of glory, we charge forward, we fight, we kill. And there are more of them, we fight on, I see Father now and then, his sword arm raised, his battle axe besmeared and I look back to see a man aiming at me. I duck, I swivel, I pierce his side and he screams as he goes down. I ride on past and go for the man following him.

Exhaustion is an enemy as much as the enemy. Arms ache unbearably, legs are forced to keep moving, back aches abominably and still they come and still they fight and even as our men and their men went down and we trampled them and stumbled over them and all but fell on them, the battle raged on. The horses screamed as they were pierced to bring down their riders, the men screamed as their life was taken at the point of a sword or dagger or smashed out of them with a battle axe. The sound was indescribable and endless. The blood-letting was savage and relentless. And in the middle of all the carnage, there was a destrier, teeth bared, hooves ready to kick the life out of anyone who came near it, ridden by the young pretender king, covered in blood from head to foot, looking as near to being demonic as any man I had ever seen.

Then Norfolk arrived with fresh troops and a great whoop went up from the Yorkist side and I knew then that the battle was done and we had lost.

In truth, though, and this is something I have said to none in 550 years, it was not the arrival of Norfolk's men which turned the battle, but the spectres who rode in with him. For sure that man was in league with the very Devil himself, for he came with dead as well as living, with skeletons astride fire breathing horses, skeletons which grinned a death grin and screamed silently for victory in the battle. Those around me took one look and began to run from the soul searing vision of ghastly bones astride horses which were not of any breed known to man – but known in the lower reaches of Hell, of a surety they were.

Norfolk's living men charged into the battle as if possessed. No normal man could look the way they did; their faces carried the same look as the skeletons who rode alongside them. Only now do I ask, were they aware of their ghostly demonic companions? Did Norfolk tell them who would ride into battle with them?

And the battle was done. Those who could run were cut down by those pursuing them. Those who escaped fell in the river and drowned. Those who did not run, Father and I were among them, were rounded up as prisoners. We stood among our fallen, surrounded by skeletal soldiers with fire in their eye sockets and no words in their silent mouths and yet oozed menace. We did not move.

I believed then we had fought our last battle, that our days were ended, that our time had come, for some were taken from the group of prisoners and executed right there, heads chopped off and thrown among the corpses. I was sick to my soul, afeared I would have to see my father executed and then follow him to my own death. So sick I almost vomited but held it back and stood proud and tall, as a Wydville had to.

To our great relief and gratitude, we were released, along with others, to find our weary horses, what men we had left and to make our way home.

Towton had been a battle never to be forgotten, then or now.

They said later 28,000 men died, they said we fought for ten hours. I believe we fought for a week, not hours. I believe there was a point in which the Lancastrians could have stood their ground, or I would like to think that, anyway, but the demons which came in with Norfolk turned the tide and began the exodus.

Even now I see the spectral figures riding into the combatants, see the grinning skulls; sense the menace that they brought with them. Even now I wake from sleep with a scream on my lips and hatred for the Devil and all who serve him in my heart.

But we do what we have to do. We asked for pardon, it was granted. We sought closer ties with the Yorkist king; we found it when he married my sister.

We hoped for happiness in our later lives, but fate proved too strong for that. In the end the Yorkists were our downfall anyway.

I never, in all the years I knew him, had the courage to ask Edward IV if he knew whether Norfolk had dealings with the devil, for fear he would laugh and call me insane. I know not to this day if he knew of the skeletal soldiers which turned the battle for him.

I know only that this is a true record of what I saw on the battlefield of Towton on the 29th March 1461. And let none call this false.

Given under the seal of Antony, Lord Scales of Newcelles and the Isle of Wight, 2nd Earl Rivers, this day in March 2011.

Wealth, Women and Power

Richard Laymon

'What are you playing?'

The suave debonair man sat down opposite Grainger, who was rapidly flicking playing cards into piles across the table.

'Patience.'

'Not something I have in abundance...' The man raised a sculpted eyebrow to show he was making a small joke. Grainger grunted and began selecting cards, red/black/red or black/red/black.

'Interesting colours, do you not think?'

What Grainger thought was that the man should go away and leave him alone. He had an appointed task and needed to get on with it before the witching hour. He did not need some smart Alec watching and putting him off, nor did he particularly want to indulge in small talk.

The club was crowded, members standing at the bar, clustered round the small tables, clinking glasses and talking loudly to impress everyone else. He wasn't impressed, either by the club or the man sharing his table – without an invite – and wished he could be a hundred miles away in some lonely roadside inn where no one knew him and where he could drink in peace.

A hand, which for a fleeting second looked remarkably like a claw, stilled his cards.

'I can release you from this, you know.'

The words were said in such a sibilant whisper it almost hurt Grainger's ears. Not only the whisper, but the words themselves. No one knew about his penance, how could they? It was between the devil and him, no one else.

'You can't.'

'I can. Do you not understand, Grainger? I can because the person who set this on you is/was one of my minions. He has since departed my realm for the lower one, I am sad to say. He was not ... how can I say this ... reliable enough for the work I gave him.'

'Does that mean ... you are ... His Satanic Majesty...' Grainger pushed his chair back, trying to show some kind of deference to the man/creature in front of him. A low chuckle, accompanied by a blast of sulphur, stopped him.

'Don't be stupid.'

Grainger blinked a few times as the man/creature went through several rapid changes, from demonic to innocent handsome, in the space of a fraction of a second. Then he was his usual slender debonair self again.

'But...'

'Enough. I have a proposition for you which, if you carry it through, will release you from this torment. How many times do you have to get a complete game done by midnight?'

'Ten.'

'Difficult.'

'Some nights I can do it fast, some nights...'

'So, come with me, Grainger, let me show you something, a way to escape this penance.'

103

Grainger stood up, expecting to walk out of the club but in a puff of smoke he and the Devil were gone, riding a thermal of warm air high above the town. He panicked but reasoned the Devil knew what he was doing. And it was rather exciting, flying over the rooftops like that, without being seen by anyone. At least, no one looked up and pointed.

They stopped abruptly on a sharply pitched roof. Grainger clung to the chimney pot, afraid of falling.

'Now, did you get everything you wanted from my minion?'

'You mean: wealth, women and power? Yes, I did.'

'So what went wrong?'

Grainger pondered the question, one he had asked himself many times. In the end he shook his head. 'I don't know. One minute all was sunshine and rainbows, the next it was 'you betrayed me' and much shouting and carrying on. I hadn't betrayed him; I had no one to betray him to! Because...'

'No one would believe you. Quite.' The Devil stared at Grainger for a moment, his fathomless eyes reflecting the darkness of the night sky. 'I think ... my minion was far gone in paranoia and I overlooked it. My error. In return for that, Grainger, I can offer you even more wealth, more women and more power, if that is your wish.'

'In return for your minion's mistake?'

'No. In return for a favour. There is someone I wish to dispose of. You are the right person to do it.'

'Who?'

'One thing at a time. First, what level of wealth, women and power are you at right now?'

'Well, lots of money in the bank, a different woman every week and control of a very big company.'

'And you would like that stepped up to...?'

Grainger released his iron grip on the chimney, wondering if he was truly hallucinating or whether this was real, very real, that he was actually being offered limitless wealth, women and power. And then wondered, briefly, why he hadn't asked for health as well, so he could enjoy the wealth, women and power. Stupid oversight, he thought. I wonder if I can ask him about that...

'You've already got my soul, so what else can I give you?'

'Commitment.'

'It's got to be big, this favour, for you to leave Hell and come and ask me yourself, sire.'

'It is.' The sardonic grin was frightening in its intensity. 'I want you to kill someone for me. But not just any old murder, a very public one.'

'What has this person done to you – or shouldn't I ask?'

The cackle was as scarily demonic as the grin. 'He reneged on a deal. No one does that. I need this to be an example to any others who might think about doing the same thing.'

Murder. That hadn't quite been what Grainger expected but the rewards ... the rewards ...

'What do you want done to this person?'

'I want him tied behind your car and dragged along the road until he is a mess of blood, flesh and bones.'

'What?!'

'You heard.' The voice had gone icy cold and Grainger shivered. Could he do such a thing? Well, perhaps he could bribe someone else to do it...

'You have to do it, my friend.'

Damn, is he reading minds as well?

'Yes.'

Grainger clung to the chimney pot again, to stop the shivers running through him finally tipping him off the roof and into the street below.

'Let me think about it. Who is it you want killed?'

'We're on his roof now.'

'We'... oh my God!'

The Devil cuffed him around the head. 'Don't blaspheme in front of me! Now you know who it is, I give you twenty four hours to make up your mind. Go ahead and you will rule the world. Say no and I will reduce you to nothing more than a vagrant on the streets. Your choice, Grainger, your choice.'

In another puff of sulphur smoke, Grainger found himself back in the club, dealing out yet another hand of patience. He still had his penance to fulfil ... or did he? The Devil had said the minion had been sent into Hell. He put the cards together and stacked them neatly in the middle of the table.

And sat staring into the middle distance.

Kill someone. Murder them by dragging them along behind his car. Very public and very nasty. Even if he did it at night, there might be witnesses. It would need careful planning.

All this reasoning was displacement activity to stop him thinking about who the victim was to be.

His best friend.

He had no idea, none whatsoever, that his friend had done a deal with the Devil, that he had reneged on that deal, that the Devil was after him, big time. But it did account for the sudden change in fortune, for the big house, big car, big busted blonde on his arm... Luck, he had said, pure luck, old man.

And Grainger realised that the roof he and the Devil had been clinging to, well, he had been clinging to, was his friend's house. The new, big, expensive house he bought with the 'luck' that had come his way.

Kill his best friend.

Lose his fortune if he didn't.

Would his friend pick him up from the streets, would his friend have time for him if he couldn't match him pound for pound, woman for woman? How much of a true 'best friend' was he? And how could he find out before committing murder?

Was he even contemplating killing someone? Seriously?

He went to the bar and began working his way through a bottle of very old brandy. By the fourth glass it might just as well have been vinegar for all the taste he had of it. He needed to get drunk and he did.

The club finally pushed him into a taxi and sent him home.

Cold sober and hung over next morning, Grainger realised that he had been given an impossible dichotomy. He could not kill his friend. He doubted he could kill anyone. And he could not live on the streets, either. He would die within a week. He had no survival skills of any kind, his

107

whole life had been one of luxury and it had got better when he had made the deal with the demon he thought was the Devil. Now, having met the 'real thing', he wondered how he could have been so mistaken. No one could measure up to the coldness, the sheer blackheartedness, as it were, of the Devil himself.

Well, it had been good, for a while. Now there was only one way out.

He spent the entire day on his computer, closing accounts, sorting out his life, writing instructions for those who would have to sort everything out. He would leave them with a huge question, why? For there had been nothing in his life to indicate unhappiness. In truth, there hadn't been, until now. He should have known that that the Devil's deals were far from straightforward.

By the evening he was ready, calm and assured. As the 24 hour deadline arrived, the Devil arrived too, as suave and debonair as before.

'Have you decided, Grainger?'

'I have.'

'And?'

'Take me back to that same roof.'

The Devil frowned. 'Is this entirely necessary? I have another meeting and you will delay me.'

'It is.'

'Then come.'

And in a moment they were on the same roof.

'This is my answer.' Grainger pushed past the Devil and allowed himself to fall the four storeys to the ground, without a sound passing his lips. By the impact alone, the Devil knew he had not survived.

'Damn and blast and heaven!' he muttered. 'Now I have to find someone else.'

Beaters

Richard Laymon

See the men come toward us in line with sticks and clubs and guns. Like a line of beaters.

See the men and know they come -

Lord Amighty but I'm that scared I could -

It was Bunce who started all this - or was it Jimmy?

Bunce. It was him who come arunning and said

"Hey guys, there's a spacemen in the woods!" and we, knowing Bunce ain't all there, you know what I mean, the lift don't always go to the top floor, like, we laughed and said: "You've been watching too much Star Trek!"

But he kept on saying, "There's a spaceman in the woods!"

It were a kinda boring day, too hot to kick footballs, torment dogs and cats, too brainstorming to go to school, so we went to the woods.

Well now, like I said, Bunce ain't got all that there is in the way of brains, so we weren't surprised when we got to the woods to find there was not a spaceman there at all.

An alien: not a spaceman.

It was kinda hard to say what he/it looked like, really, green and scaly and like nothing on earth and then it was changing shape, first grey and smoky like my old Dad's pipe smoke, then sort of like a tree, then sort of like a large polecat, then sort of like -

Jimmy.

That's when I got a bit scared and backed off a bit but it spoke with Jimmy's voice and kinda sounded sad and lonely-like.

"Stay with me," and it was kinda hard to go, then. Bunce and Jimmy and me, we stared at it for a while and walked round it and it looked more like Jimmy every minute till even Jimmy was taken to say,

"Damn it all, whoever you be, you looks just like the twin brother I never had!"

"But you don't like me as I am," and it sounded even more lonely, like an old train whistling across the countryside in the middle of the night, rushing headlong to - Nowheresville.

And you feel your heart sort of sink in your boots and you want to go and cry into some bale of straw or sommat.

Then it became Bunce. Just like that, in a twinkle of a will o' the wisp apassing us by, it became Bunce.

And then they were astaring and pointing because it became me.

And I got real scared.

"We'd better get going, guys!" I took off running, fast as I could, sweat apouring under the arms and everywhere, heading for home.

"Dad!" I yelled, knowing damn well him were asleeping off the old moonshine somewhere on the back porch but not caring if I got a licking or not. Somehow it didn't matter.

"Dad!" and he woke and shook the porch with thumping feet and yelled enough to bring down the old lightning struck elm outside.

"What is it, boy? This had damn well better be good!"

And I told him about the alien and how it was first Jimmy then Bunce and then me and how it stared and cried and made us feel all lonely.

"There be no such thing as an alien, boy," he spoke kinda slow and serious. "That there be the work of the Devil himself. I'll just go and see old Sam, downalong," and him peg legged off down the dirt track, raising dust devils of his own.

Good, I thought, the men will come and kill the creature!

Then I got thinking about Bunce and Jimmy and how the alien looked like them and how the men wouldn't know who they be ashooting and I got even more scared and ran back as fast as I could, stitch cutting my side into pieces and gasping like I was a marathon runner done the 26 miles without stopping even for a coke along the way and found three people sat at the foot of the old oak where it was once said a man done hung himself after a love affair went wrong and we thought how stupid to do that.

And I was thinking round in a circle because the three who sat at the foot of the tree were -

Identical.

And something reached out and touched me, I felt cat's paws of tickling all over my head my back my stomach my legs and I felt myself changing and changing and changing -

Into Bunce.

Now we were four.

Work of the Devil.

Satan's children.

No one would believe we were victims of an outer space creature now, would they?

See the men come toward us in line with sticks and clubs and guns. Like a line of beaters.

See the men and know they come -

Lord Amighty but I'm that scared I could –

I Ain't Got No Body

Richard Laymon

It's that damned piano thing underwriting the song, trilling through the instrumental bits, ornamenting the gee-tars – doesn't everyone say it that way? – wrapping around the sax, you know what I mean. Gets me every damn time. Memories. Music's a time machine, one hint of an intro and you're right back there, staring at whatever it is that struck you at that time; love, hate, drama, death and destruction, melancholy, the music takes you straight back, doesn't it?

I'm only the cleaner at Pharaoh's nightclub here in Portsmouth, but I do like to slink back in from time to time, sit at the end of the bar with a drink or three and watch the performances, on the dance floor and off. Tarquin, the boss man, gave me a pass so I didn't have to pay, the 'doormen' don't know me as I usually go in out of hours, when they're flat out on their comfy beds snoring the night's excess away.

Tarquin was good to me. Now that's a stupid statement considering I did much more than clean the place for him. I cleaned him at times, in a manner of speaking. Don't ask me why I got the pleasure when there were hookers galore but he didn't go for them, didn't seem to want the glamour and fake personalities; said he liked me because I wasn't like them. The pay was excellent, better than cleaning rates any time. Now don't you go thinking

114

I did it for the money, although I have to say it was a big part of it, I genuinely liked the guy. And he was good, which made it even better.

The best bit, though, is sitting at the bar, ignoring the looks from the men and brushing off the occasional – and I do mean occasional – invitations and listening to the piano man tinkling his way through the songs.

Until he starts on one that brings those memories back.

You noticed that I used the past tense for Tarquin, right? I doubted that was his real name, bit too posy for him in truth, but it sounded flash and he was all about flash. He was much given to flaunting himself around the club, chatting with the ones who threw their money about more than the ones who drank two-three cocktails and made them last all evening. Fair enough, his club, he does as he wishes, but he didn't see the looks he got when he did that. Me, ensconced in my corner, could see far more than he did and I knew that for some people, that was an insult. Like, wasn't their money good enough for him? What if they couldn't go with the champagne and all the rest of the high spending stuff? They were still customers and they were still entitled to have the boss man speak to them occasionally.

Tarquin was too much of a snob to do that.

So there we were, me cleaning and 'doing' and he making money hand over fist and not all of it ending up in the bank, don't you know.

And him and me having a right good time of it, don't you know, in his bed, in his study, in his bath ... we tried it everywhere and everywhere was good.

Miss it like hell, I do.

Anyway, onward.

He dropped a bombshell one night and I do mean a bombshell. He said he was thinking of marrying me.

Me. Little old me. OK, I had some looks but they didn't equal the foxy women who prowled the club. He said he didn't want that. I asked him when we could talk about it properly, it being close on time to hit the bed at that moment, and he said 'tomorrow.'

I said, fine, good, talk with you tomorrow, love you (which was a bit of a lie but still... glad I said it) and left.

And 'tomorrow' I went to work as usual.

And walked into a bloodbath.

There's this bigger than 'life size' model of Anubis in the main room. Don't I know it; I clean the damn thing every day.

Someone had taken the head off it and replaced it with Tarquin's head which was dripping blood all down the body and onto the floor.

Now the odd thing is I didn't freak out. I stared at it for a while, found myself uselessly thinking, where the hell is Anubis' head then?

Then I thought, where's the rest of Tarquin?

I know, I should have called the police there and then but hell, I was in shock and I wanted to find the rest of my fiancé, if only to prove to myself he was really dead and this was not some elaborate hoax.

I walked away from his staring eyes and twisted sort of smile and went looking for the other parts of the body.

You tell me why I started with the till – I don't know, don't suppose you do either, but there you are and there you go. Someone, the 'someone' who killed Tarquin, had the most macabre sense of humour imaginable. Tarquin's hands were in the till. What does that tell you? Right, someone right smart and on the ball knew what he was at with the takings.

OK, that was the hands. I didn't touch them, left them there, blood and all and went looking for the feet. Had the oddest feeling I knew where I'd find them and I did, in front of the urinal where he had stood so many times and compared his tackle with the customers' – often disparagingly, only to me, mind you, only to me. I wonder who knew about that.

There was no body. No arms, no legs, no torso. Nothing. About then I thought it best I called the police who came with sirens and funny yellow and black tape and men in white head to foot coverall things and they walked and talked and took pictures and shut the club up tighter than –

My lips, as it happened. I had by then got my sticky mitts on the secret stash of cash Tarquin had tucked away upstairs. He'd shown me where it was one night when he was blind drunk and I hadn't forgotten it. I might have been upset, distraught you might say but I wasn't daft and out of my head. I had my future to take care of. Pharaoh's was fit to be shut down for good after this, unless the gawkers wanted to come and stare at the place where the head was displayed and they might at that. I held that thought...

Good job I got the money out when I did, they took his room apart. Found nothing. Not so much as a grain of cocaine or a whiff of cannabis. Tarquin didn't do it. None of it. Didn't drink too much either.

Found out then that was his real name. That was a bit of a shock, I truly thought he'd given it to himself to sound good. All the time it was real. I wondered for a moment what he'd been through at school with a fancy-dancy name like that. Whatever it was, he didn't deserve to end up in bits in his own club with half of him missing.

Most of him missing.

In the end it seemed old Tarquin did me a fair favour. I had a ton of cash which I used to buy the club with no questions asked by anyone, not after told them I'd had an inheritance – which was as true as it comes, wasn't it? They never did find the rest of him then, even though I ordered a coffin big enough to take it all when or if it ever turned up and they never pinned the murder on anyone, either. No evidence, see?

Should be sitting pretty, shouldn't I? Tarquin no more than a fond memory, me the proud owner of a thriving nightclub and the attention of some rather tasty guys, now I have property and a position in society.

The problem is; we have a new piano man. He doesn't know what I like and what I don't like, what I asked the piano man not to play – like ever. I forgot to tell this one. You get used to someone sat there tinkling away and you don't think they might go do what you don't want them to do. If you get my meaning.

So I am here this night, sitting with my drink at the bar, thinking about poor old Tarquin and how awful he looked with his head on the wooden body of old Anubis over there – and right glad I am I don't do the cleaning these days – when the piano man launches into that old classic, 'I Ain't Got Nobody' and there's me, tears in my eyes, hearing it – as I always did - as 'I Ain't Got No Body.'

It reminded me of the time I needed to get someone in to check out the awful smell in the drains out back of the men's toilets. It was getting pretty bad in there.

119

Night Feeds

Richard Laymon

"Leanne, the door is unlocked."

"So?"

"You said you locked it when you went to bed."

"I did."

"Damn it, the door was UNLOCKED!"

"Don't shout at me! I locked it!"

Dan stood there, hands on hips, radiating anger through every pore. "Were you sleepwalking again?"

Leanne laughed and pulled the duvet back over her head. "How the hell would I know?"

"I don't understand." Anger was replaced by bafflement. "How can you walk and not know it?"

"How can you toss and turn in your sleep and not know it?"

"We've been here before, Lee, I don't understand it, never will."

"Sorry. I can't help it. You're acting like I do it on purpose." She lowered the duvet and stared at his much loved face and haunted eyes. His look changed suddenly into something knowing and – devious.

"Is this – diagnosed, this sleepwalking? I mean, does anyone else know about it?"

Leanne sat up, staring at him. "Why?"

"Well..."

"You planning on using it in some way, Dan?"

"Well..."

"It's a brilliant idea!" She got out of bed, ran across the room and hugged him. "We need a new supply, why didn't we think of that before?"

"Been too busy working out how to keep the damn door locked," he sighed into her hair. "How am I going to stop you unlocking the door, Lee?"

"No idea," she mumbled into his broad chest. "Have to hope any wannabe burglar doesn't choose our home above all the others in the street, is all."

"No, because with what I have in mind, we wouldn't want the police round here..."

She grinned. "No, we wouldn't, would we?"

It was as if they had a combined mind at that moment, they both 'saw' the body of the vagrant stored in their coal shed. The door of that was tight locked and Leanne had no idea where the key was. Some things Dan could not take a chance on, no matter what. Burglary, yes, they could just about get away with that, but if there was a hint that anyone knew of their nocturnal activities...

"You can just wander the streets, looking as if you're asleep, Lee. You spot the potentials, I'll do the rest. Anyone stops you, you're sleep-walking."

"Save us a lot of worry, Dan, won't it? All this 'waiting for someone to call' business, doesn't work well enough for my liking."

"Nor mine. Get dressed, Lee, let's go eat. I'm starving and the tramp should be about ready by now, soft enough to chew."

"I need a nightshirt, Dan."
"Why?"

"You're really not thinking this through, are you? Sleepwalkers don't get dressed before they go out! I need to go out as I would be dressed for bed."

"But you don't dress for bed."

"You want me to walk the streets naked, then, do you?"

"No ..." He rubbed his hair into a disgrace. "I don't know ... I didn't want it to cost money."

"Hard luck. I need to walk the streets in something, that something can't be jeans and tee-shirt, or dress or – can it?"

"No. OK, I'll get you one. What size?"

"A ten. Nothing bigger, thanks. They come up large as it is."

When Dan had gone, Leanne sat and stared out of the small grubby window at the small grubby world opposite. Rows of terraced houses glared back at her, resenting the implied criticism of the unwatered window boxes, unpainted doors and uncared for gardens, if you could call them that.

"I wish we could leave here," she whispered to the glass, which ignored her, of course. It had its own job to do, keeping the outside world out and the inside world in. She laughed, what nonsensical thoughts were playing on her mind! It was the anticipation, the mere thought of going out on the streets in a charade of somnambulism with murder at the end of it. Murder. It was much more fun than waiting for some tramp to knock and then quietly smothering him with a feather pillow.

And that's not murder? A little voice questioned from somewhere in the depths of her mind. No, that's mercy killing. Who wants to be a tramp, a vagrant, a burden on the goodness of society?

Not like murder. Not like enticing someone back, someone thinking they're helping the sufferer and then –pounce! Now that *will* be fun!

Excited shivers ran the length of her body at the mere thought.

Then she returned to her earlier wish, that they could leave. But where could they find a place which had a convenient coal shed which could be tripled locked against her lock picking abilities during her sleepwalking, where they could entice the vagrants and store them, where they could dispose of the rotting bodies when they were done – the amount of places you can hide parts of bodies was amazing, when you knew the area well. To move would mean starting over again with all that knowledge and what would they live on in the meantime?

Dan was coming down the road, carrying a small carrier bag. Had he done it, got the right kind of night shirt, the right size? If he had, it would be a first ... she ran to open the door for him.

"Hurry up and show me!" she demanded, anxiously eyeing the bag. He opened it and shook out a bright pink garment embroidered with kittens. Totally innocuous. "I love it!" she squealed and held it up against her. "Thank you, darling!" He leaned over for a kiss which developed into an all out session and ended up with them rolling around the floor.

"I love you, Leanne," he said finally, looking down at the tousled flushed girl beneath him on the floor. "I would do anything for you."

"Same goes for me to you, beloved."

"Tonight then?"

"Tonight. With the sour taste of the tramp in our mouths and the singing of his rusting blood in our veins, we will seek fresh supplies!"

And they did. They entrapped and they conquered and they fed on clean new meat and uncontaminated blood. And they loved and laughed and sang until dawn about how easy it was to lead someone home when all you had to do was pretend to be asleep and on the street. How gullible people were!

And they fell asleep in each other's arms.

Leanne woke at twilight, reaching for Dan but he wasn't there. Gone for something to drink, perhaps, she thought dully. She swung her legs out of bed and looked down at the floor where her new nightshirt lay, covered in blood.

"What the hell..."

She hadn't done any killing – that she knew of. They had smothered the new meat, to keep it fresher. No blood-letting. Where had this come from?

"Dan?"

She searched the apartment and found no sign of him. No sign he had even been there.

"Dan?" A rising note of hysteria as she felt the sense of enormous loss. Had he left her?

There was only one place left to look and it was impossible – absolutely out of this world impossible – that he was there but she had to look, she had to be satisfied she had searched everywhere. She grabbed his towelling robe from the hook behind the door, tied the belt tightly round her waist and

124

crept outside, afraid of the sunshine, the neighbours, the neighbourhood. Leanne was a night person through and through. Sunlight scorched her blood and crinkled up her eyes.

She held the key to the coal shed in her hand.

She wondered how she knew where it was. Dan had gone to great lengths to hide it from her.

She crept to the door of the shed and opened the lock. It gave way easily under her skilful fingers. *I've done this before.*

Inside was the body of the Good Samaritan she had enticed home the night before.

On top of the body was what was left of Dan.

Letters I've Written...

Charles L Grant

Do you not keep your love letters? Do you not read them in the dead of night, in the time when all life is stilled, when breathing is shallow and thoughts are deep, when light is dimmed and hopes go with it into the darkness? Do you not then reach for the lamp and illuminate your heart and your room, do you not reach for the letters in their secret box concealed under your bed, where you hope against all hope no one will think to look for them?

What if they do?

What will they discover? Your endless outpourings of love for those who are no longer in your life? The pain your heart went through, embedded in the warp and weft of the paper on which your words are immortalised? Do you think they will laugh at you if they read them? Or would they empathise to the point when sorrow takes over and they weep over the letters, knowing that their life is writ clear there too?

Ignore that. We are talking of you reaching for the letters in the darkest reaches of the night, the endless depressing unbearably lonely night, when you hold the letters and touch them and smell them and remember them, word for word.

Remember Harriet, the blonde with the nose which wrinkled when she laughed? The eyes which twinkled no matter what mood she seemed to be in? Harriet, who laughed at the wrong times and the

126

right times, who was slender and graceful and delightful to be with?

For the moment, put her memory, affectionately, to one side and let us move on to Georgina, the elegant, leggy sultry dark haired girl with the penchant for foreign cigarettes, preferably Russian, for strange cocktails and equally strange men to go with them. She was good for a time, wasn't she?

Melissa, oh how could you forget Melissa ...

How many in all? Do you remember?

Count the letters and you will.

One by one, smell and touch and remember.

Each one is different, is it not?

Each one is written in the blood of the victim.

Before they died.

Keeping The Ghosts Away

Bela Lugosi

"Boxer, how many times do I have to say it? Close the defences!"

"Why? They'll get in, no matter what we do!"

"Because ... oh to hell with it. OK, I'll close the defences for you."

"It don't matter. We're gonners anyway. Ain't we?"

"Not if we fight back."

"What do we wanna do that for?"

Scott sighed. "Because..." he began and then stopped. Boxer would never understand. You just didn't give in because giving in was for losers. He wasn't a loser. If Boxer wanted to walk out there and let them eat him up, that was his choice. On the other hand if he did, he, Scott, would lose his right hand person for – well, everything, supplies, water, manning the barricades... the thought was not tenable. Barney was out back, but Barney was pretty much a robot, tell him what to do, set him walking and talking and then tell him when to stop again. Not much help when they were under attack.

Boxer stood, hands loose at his side, a slack look to his face, off in his own Boxer world once again.

"Hey, snap to, fella, we have things to do! Food, for a start. I'm near starving."

Boxer seemed to come out of a dream and into the real world again with difficulty. "All right, Scottie, all right. I'll rustle up sommat for you."

"Good. You do that and I'll see to everything else."

Barney strolled in, bland face as usual, if any thoughts ever really went on in that head, Scott had yet to find them. Even a hint of them.

"We eating soon, Scotts?"

"Boxer's rustling up sommat, he says. I'm sealing the defences. We'll be safe for a while."

"Ok, Scotts, no probs. Gotta rest, so tired. Old legs are weary."

Scott looked round in alarm. This wasn't Barney's way at all, he had boundless energy and –

Oh hell and damnation. He was growing visibly fainter by the second.

"Boxer! Get in here fast!"

Boxer came charging in, waving a spatula in one hand, ready to shout some sarcastic comment or other when he looked at Barney and stopped in his tracks. "Oh shit."

"Right! Get him outside, quick as you can!"

Boxer tossed the spatula onto the table, scooped up the fast fading Barney and ran for the window. He levered the catch up with one hand and then dropped their one time friend outside. The howls of the approaching ghosts warned him he was just in time.

We reclaim our own! We reclaim our own!

"Like hell you do," snarled Scott, smearing butter round the edges of the window frame once it was tight shut. "See how you try getting past that, you filthy spooks!"

Shrieks sounded from the semi-darkness as one ghost after another tried the window and was repelled by the grease. "That'll hold them for a

129

while," Scott said grimly. He looked at Boxer. "Sorry, old mate, I know he was your friend but they got him, didn't they?"

Boxer sat down at the table, looking utterly disconsolate. "Barney was all right, Scott, really he was. A bit vacant, perhaps, but good hearted and worked hard, didn't he? Damned if I know when they got him. I thought he was safe with us." He looked up, rueful. "Now I see why you keep on about defences. Sure, they'll get us eventually but before then, we have to fight on, don't we?"

"I'm not giving up and walking out there, Box, that's for sure. They can come get me if they like, I ain't giving up to them."

"So, what we gotta do, Scottie?"

"Get every nook and cranny buttered. Like every last one. I need to get up in the roof, seal it up there, then down the cellar, seal it down there, then the walkway to the barn, seal all that."

"What shall I do, Scottie?"

"Cook me some food. I need to eat!"

"Sure, course. Damn, I left it all when you called me. There'll be a lot over now, I was-"

"I know, can't be helped. It's you and me now, old mate, you and me. We'll be all right, you see."

If there was enough butter to go round everywhere he needed to put it, that was. Otherwise his days were numbered, too. But he had to try, for the sake of any others out there who were also keeping the ghosts away, he had to try. One day they could join forces and defeat this persistent vigilant and successful enemy. He wondered if others knew about the butter ...

Then decided it didn't matter if they did or not. He did and he had to do something about it.

"Food in about ten minutes!" Boxer shouted from the kitchenette. Not long enough to get in the roof space and do anything. Not long enough to tackle the walkway. Enough time to re-seal the front door, though, he was sure he could hear someone touching the knocker.

He hurried into the hall just in time to see the movement as a figure moved away from the door. Yes, they were trying it, but double glazing was very effective, even without the sealant.

More butter caused a howling noise as if souls were being tormented, or was that in his head? Whatever, if it was hurting them, it was good.

He hurried back into the lounge in time to take a plate of food from Boxer. "Thanks, mate!"

They sat forking food into their mouths, silent in their hunger, lost in their own memories of poor old Barney, wondering if he was part of the silent crowd pressing against the glass as if by pressure they could force their way through and grab them both.

Finally Boxer sighed and put his plate down. "I can't stop thinking about him. He looked so – thin!"

"I know. Scary, isn't it, how you go when they get their claws into you?"

"Nothing there. Nothing there at all. I held him with one arm while I got the window open."

"I know."

"If you like, I'll tackle the roof space if you want to do the walkway. The barn's secure, isn't it?"

"Too right. They're not getting any of our animals, Box!"

"Right, I'll do that then. I'll sleep easier tonight if I know the roof's done."

"Thanks, mate, I do appreciate that more than I can tell you. I've had enough of this, so I'll start on the walkway. Thanks, by the way, good food there."

"Well..." Boxer ducked his head, embarrassed by praise. "Not much but it does, don't it?"

"Surely does. Right..."

It took him an hour to seal the walkway, an hour during which he was aware of being stalked on the other side by unseen but very obvious beings, hearing their muttering, their threats; their entreaties to put it all aside and go out and join them. He ignored all of it, singing a folk song under his breath, repeating it endlessly as a mantra until they fell back and let him get on with it.

Back in the house, he climbed the ladder to the loft space to see how Boxer was getting on. He had done really well, every tiny crevice had been effectively sealed and he was busy with the chimney, making doubly sure there was no way they could get in there. The heavy slab which Scott had put up there was being sealed into position with mastic and then more butter.

"Hey, Scottie, why does butter work?" he asked, resting his weary arms.

"Don't know. My great grandmother told me about it when I was big enough to stand by her knee. I never forgot it."

"Was she American?"

"No, Hungarian."

"Oh, vampires and all that."

"Right on. Vampires and all that. She had a remedy for everything that came out of the darkness at you and then some. All of it's up here somewhere-" He tapped the side of his head. "It comes out when I need it, not otherwise."

"Any chance you know how we're gonna get out of this mess eventually, Scottie?"

"Not yet. One thing at a time. First we stay safe, then we get out of here."

"Fine by me. Only we'll go stir crazy and end up doing their job for them if we stay too long."

Scott grinned at his friend in the semi-darkness of the roof space. "Oh I know, Box, I know..."

They shook hands, a sudden burst of emotion which embarrassed them both. Scott put it down to the loss of Barney just that short time before, a Barney who was there and then not there. Damn the spooks! Taking his friend like that! I'll get you! he vowed silently.

The two men climbed down into the house and went to the barn together. The animals called softly when they walked in, looking for food, for milking, for comfort of men. No doubt the ghosts had been bothering them, but the barn was well sealed, Scott had made sure of that.

He and Boxer worked together in companionable silence. The comforting noise of the animals shifting and muttering to one another, the sound of their chomping on feed, the rustle as they went about their work, made a gentle backdrop against which they could hear the howling of the demented ghosts, determined to find a way in. Tomorrow they would find the battered empty shells where they had knocked so hard against the walls trying to get in they had died.

They would count the corpses and rejoice.

Later, back in the house with a bottle of rare fine old brandy between them, Scott looked across at his friend and smiled.

"Thanks, Box, you were great."

Boxer shuffled and looked away. "Nothin', Scottie. Sommat we had to do. What's the plans for the future, then? Got any?"

"Yeah, I have, as it happens. I want to get into town, get into the library, but to do that I need a suit they can't get through."

"What you want in town?"

"Information. There's gotta be a way to fight back, Box, I gotta get on line or get the old books or get – I don't know, whatever it takes to find out how to fight the spooks. Perhaps we can link up with others, see what they're doing, see if we can raise an army, wipe them out."

"Wish we could eat them."

"I wish that too, Box. Save us a lot of problems looking for fresh kills, wouldn't it?"

Boxer grinned. "Been a while, Scottie, how long can we hold out?"

Scott contemplated the freezer and the flasks stacked in the cellar, did some calculations and looked thoughtful. "Well, now there's only two of us, the blood will last a lot longer. I reckon we can hold till Spring before we need new supplies. In an emergency... we could have a little from the animals, but it isn't the same."

"I know, but – well, I guess it's one positive thing about old Barney going then."

"Sure is." Scott yawned, stood up and began to move toward the stairs. "I'll sleep better today for

134

all the work we did, Box. You should, too. See you at nightfall, then."

"G'day to you, Scottie."

Scott slowly climbed the stairs, wondering if he was capable of at least cleaning his fangs before he settled down to sleep, then decided against it. He was shattered.

Let the ghosts do their worst, he thought, as he slid the coffin lid to one side. I don't care. They can't reach me and Box now and we have time to work out how to fight back. Wonder if they know they're up against a couple of vampire ghost fighters?

Too bad if they don't.

The lid slid back into position with a gentle thump.

Scott was asleep in two minutes.

Crossroads Blues

Richard Laymon

Hey, thanks! Been walking that road forever, breathing everyone's fumes and not one cared to stop for me. Damn thumb near enough aching from being stuck out so long and being ignored, too!

This is one fine car, I have to say. Nice. What's the music ... oh, OK, never mind. I can live with it.

What? What do I like? Blues. Old style blues. Let me tell you a story, then, how I got to be where I was when you picked me up, you being a damn fine person and all, let me tell you. You up for that?

Well, like I said, I like the blues and I had this ambition, you know? Man, did I ever want to sing the blues! You know, like the old 'uns, none of this wailing guitars and sobbing violins and screaming keyboards ... anyone can make a blues song outta that. No, me and the old guitar, a voice and a song and a heartbreak, that's what I wanna do. Like Robert Johnson, like Blind Lemon Jefferson, like the Reverend Gary Davis ... they didn't need no backing, did they?

So there I was, sat in the park – 'cos the family done got sick of me plucking the same chords over and over and I got jokes like 'I didn't wake up this morning' and stuff like that – crooning to myself about lost loves and too much drink and roads that go on forever especially when you're walking them, when this guy strolls up to me. Smooth like, slicked back hair, slicked back clothes, come to think on it and shiny shoes like they just came out of the box but he walked like they were slippers. That shouted money to me, you gotta spend a lot of money to get new shoes that soft and well fitting. I just drooled over the shoes.

Yeah, I know, supposed to be the females who are shoeaholics, but I do like a good pair of shoes and I had ambitions, oh yes, to go buy me handmade soft leather shoes one of these days, when the right person finds me and promotes me and I sell records by the million …

You gotta have a dream, aintcha?

And here he was, the dream, right in front of me.

'Cos this here guy says, in a voice as slicked back as his hair, 'you got something there, son, I'd like to hear more.' Before I could answer, he snaps open a silver box like you'd keep smokes in but thinner, you know what I mean? And out comes a smart piece of card, embossed with silver and all, wouldn'cha know. Record Producer it said. His name? Don't ask, I didn't see. When you want a recording more than you want the next breath, well, sort of, who sees names? You see what you wants to see. I saw Record Producer. My heart near enough stopped in its rhythm, that it did.

The funny thing is, now I think on it, he never got impatient, no shuffling of feet in those fine leather shoes, no sigh of impatience as I stilled my heart and my thinking and my sudden desire to gush madly all over the place which wouldn't have been good, now would it, who wants syncophatic gushing, I ask you...

So I got myself together and I said, calmly and quietly, like, 'thank you, sir. I would really appreciate a chance to show the world what I can do.'

'Oh you will,' he said, so quiet like I wasn't sure I heard him. Even more slicked back than before. I started to think he was all oil inside, he was that smooth, that liquid, that – do you know, the word gloopy comes to mind? Now why would that be, I wonder?

So we goes for a drink, like, he ordering some fancy cocktail the like of which I'd never heard nor seen before and man, having seen how it looked in the glass, all sort of fiery and wild and dark and menacing – now there's another odd thing, menacing? A drink? well, it was, and right glad I was I asked for a straight pint. I know where I am with beer. You can keep the fancy stuff. He tossed the drink back and went and got another. Then I got to look at him proper like for the first time.

You know how some people's eyes are so black they show nothing? No? Well, that was how his looked to me. Couldn't read a thing in them, not a thing. Worried me a bit but I kept thinking 'record producer' and tried to overlook the almost blank face, the expressionless eyes, the cut of a mouth – hardly any lips, you see – and concentrated on the oily slicked back voice, which was talking of demo discs, of expensive recording time for free, of introductions to top people, of air play and of money.

'What do you want of me?' I asked eventually. Nothing comes free, there's always a price.

'Ha, about time you asked that.' There was an edge to the voice that hadn't been there before. I sat up a bit and wondered why the change.

138

'Well ... nothing is free, is it, not really...'

'A wise person, for a change. You're right, friend, nothing is free. I don't want much of you, actually. I would ask that the first recording we make be out in the open, is all, with a hand held recorder, we can clean it up later, be assured of that, but I want real blues, dirty down low and gutsy blues, I want – you to come to the crossroads at midnight and sing for me.'

Do you know, I fell for it? How stupid is that? You can ask yourself that question as I did and get no answer. It was the oily voice, you see, which held glittering promises in its depth, bit like oil that's spilled shows up as a rainbow. That kind of thing.

Damn me if I didn't go. The crossroads he specified were miles from anywhere, my beat up old car only just made it before it coughed its last and expired in a heap of rust right there on the side of the road. I had just pulled over in time. I got out, guitar rescued from the back seat, song in my head and my mouth, and went over to the crossroads – where he was waiting.

I still didn't fall in with knowledge, you know. Even though I had his card in my pocket and wondered why he spelled Damon as Daemon.

He had this fancy recording thing in his hand. I felt pretty damn stupid, standing at a crossroads singing a blues about standing at a crossroads, a sort of interpretation of Robert Johnson's which I rather liked, but then I got into the spirit of it, sang my heart out and all but made my fingers bleed on the guitar strings.

He said I did just fine, it was exactly what he wanted. He said he would get in touch with me. I said thanks, don't you want to write down my name and address and stuff? No, he said, I know where you live and he reeled off my address, my phone number, my mobile number, my security information ... man it were scary, I tell you.

I ain't been the same since. Something's gone out of me. Now I don't believe in this soul thing, but there might be a grain of truth in it, since I sang that song and stood on that crossroads, I feel different.

Empty.

Did I hear from him again? No.

What am I doing hitching? Trying to get back to the crossroads to see if I can get it back, whatever 'it' is.

Not holding out a lot of hope but hey, thanks for the ride. This is one lonely old road when you have to walk it.

The crossroads are right here.

Don't fancy staying with me, do you?

Thought not.

Waiting for the 9.03

Edith Wharton

There is nothing as heart-breaking as a train whistle at midnight across a desolate lonely countryside. Nothing tears at the heartstrings quite as much as the sight of the brightly lit windows making a streak of light as the train clacks and rocks its way along the glittering rails.

Nothing draws the wanderlust out of the soul of someone more than the thought of the train travelling through the night to far off places where the people are different and colourful, where the food is exotic and the weather erratic and hot, where the language is like molten silver in the ears and you cannot understand a word of it.

Nothing is more lonely than standing on the platform of a deserted station and feeling the ground vibrate as the midnight train races through without so much as a nod toward a place where it once stopped to let people off, let people on and to top up with water and coal.

It's been a long, long time since a steam train went through here. I know, I have stood here many a long year watching for the steam and smoke rising above the horizon, hearing the clicking of the rail that said 'I'm coming/I'm coming' and it was, in all its heat and noise and steam and coal dust glory. But no more.

I stand on the platform and dream of days gone by Days of steam and fashion, of porters and guards, of slamming doors and shining wheels that sing their message as they click and clack their way down the lines that lead to – anywhere else but here.

And I play, 'do you remember...'

Many a year ago I came here day by day to board the 9.03 train for London and work and people and bustle and taxis and everything. So sophisticated, stiletto heels and bucket bag, those huge handbags we all carried at that time, stuffed with everything the girl about town needed, including a book. Everyone carried a book or a paper. It was not done to speak on a train; you buried yourself in the words and did not look at your fellow passengers. The great engines huffed into the station, metal dragons tamed by man, all steam and smoke and coal dust. With much slamming of doors we would climb aboard, find a seat if we were lucky, hang from a strap or the overhead luggage rack if we were not, book in the other hand, immersed in the words. Outside the whistles and slams went on, the last minute passengers running for a compartment, any compartment, until the final blast and the dragon found its breath to carry on its journey.

It was on one of those days I saw her. She was standing at the very end of the platform, alone, lonely. I wondered all day why I thought she was lonely. She was wearing vaguely old fashioned clothes, as if she had come from another time almost, but that was stupid, wasn't it?

Wasn't it?

I looked for her when the long frantic people crushed day was over and I got out of the train. She wasn't there. Had she got tired, or had the person she was waiting for actually arrived and they had gone off somewhere? My imagination was working overtime. I created all manner of stories over the weeks that followed, all wild and wonderful and no doubt every one of them a million miles from the truth.

Then I saw her again. Same clothes, same sad face, same point on the platform. I wanted to speak to her, to find out why she stood there, what she wanted but the crush carried me onto the train and London-bound before I could get near her. If I had, what would she have thought of a stranger asking such personal questions?

The biggest question of all was; why was she getting to me?

As we – I say we meaning that dragon puffing steam and coal dust and the motley collection of commuters being dragged along behind in carriages that were close to being cattle trucks – came into the station, I realised what was getting to me.

The woman was my twin.

If I was to go to a 'vintage' shop and buy a similar outfit and stand next to her on the platform, no one would be able to tell us apart.

The thought was scary.

I looked for her day after day. She wasn't there. I went to work feeling oddly empty, something missing, something needed filling and only she could do that.

But I didn't know who she was. How could someone I didn't know be responsible for my feeling empty and lonely and lost?

How could someone I didn't know look so much like me?

143

It was about that time I began to change my clothes. It wasn't a conscious decision; it was just that the clothes the woman wore seemed more attractive to me than the mini-skirts, tight tops, stilettos and everything I had been wearing.

The people on the platform, the people on the train, hardly gave me a second glance when I wore the different clothes and it was about then I realised that as commuters we were all anonymous. The only thing which had character was the train itself, the huge puffing dragon which towed us back and forth from our station.

The 'modern' clothes were discarded, binned, handed in to the charity shop, depending on the state of them at the time. The wardrobe became filled with 20s clothes, elegant, pastel coloured suits and beautiful blouses, the small hat perched on a new (to me) hairstyle that suited the suits better. Flowing dresses with long strings of beads. I looked more like the woman on the platform than ever before. It bothered me and yet it felt right.

I saw her again one morning as I was waiting for the 9.03. She smiled and gestured to me to walk over to her. I did, pushing my way through the commuters who turned away in their studied indifference to my passing them by, jostling their papers and briefcases, brushing against their arms or back. I was all but invisible.

She smiled widely when I reached her and held out her arms. Without thinking I walked into her embrace.

And changed places with her.

I watched her walk back to my place on the platform, watched the steam announce the arrival of the 9.03, saw her climb on board with a smile for the man who stood back to let her get on first.

I've been here ever since.

Nothing is more lonely than standing on the platform of a deserted station and feeling the ground vibrate as the midnight train races through without so much as a nod toward a place where it once stopped to let people off, let people on and to top up with water and coal.

It's been a long, long time since a steam train went through here. I know, I have stood here many a long year watching for the steam and smoke rising above the horizon, hearing the clicking of the rail that said 'I'm coming/I'm coming' and it was, in all its heat and noise and steam and coal dust glory. But no more.

I stand on the platform and dream of days gone by Days of steam and fashion, of porters and guards, of slamming doors and shining wheels that sing their message as they click and clack their way down the lines that lead to – anywhere else but here.

And I play, 'do you remember...'

When I looked for the arrival of the 9.03 and saw a woman out of time standing on the platform waiting, waiting, waiting...

Just A Small Thing

Richard Laymon

It was such a small thing - so small as to be almost overlooked. The shame of it is that it was not overlooked really.

Well, you asked, you came to talk to me about this, did you not? Now don't try to cover it up, don't I know that as an old, old lady with only one story to tell, there be no other reason for you to ring my doorbell?

Well now, damn, there I go again, repeating myself. Blame it on being old and having no one else to talk to, you sort of end up repeating everything to yourself. Oh yes, you're young enough not to understand, but you will. I don't know too much about the 'death and taxes' thing, I prefer to say old age and government catch up with everyone eventually. Don't you agree?

Anyway, now you're here, let me make you some tea. I get few chances these days to bring out that nice tea set, so forgive me if I go clatter and rattle in my kitchen for a while. There's magazines over there if you want to have a look at something while you're waiting.

There you go, fresh tea, fresh milk, now that's something that always amuses me. The silly supermarkets say 'fresh milk' as if they're doing us a favour. Like we would buy stale milk! Like I said, silly people.

146

I think the biscuits are fresh, too, don't know because I can't eat them. Wheat intolerance, wouldn't you know.

Right, now you've got your tea, let's talk about the 'little thing', shall we? You know it was small, everyone does. But what's small? Everyone would have a different idea on that, wouldn't they? Well, it wasn't a pea size, it was smaller than that, about half the size if I had to guess. Dark it was, no, can't give you a colour, it changed every time I looked at it. There are some crystals like that, tilt them one way and then another and they give off different colours. This thing was just like that. Bothered me no end that I couldn't work out what colour it was. No reason, just that I like to know what things are.

Where did it come from? Now you're asking. I don't know. You see, I like things nice and tidy, yes I have a few bits around the place, boxes I like, things like that, but they are all tidy and dust free. I might be old, but I know how to keep the place clean. You see, oh, sorry, doing it again, old lady habit, you'll just have to go along with me, I think. Well there I was picking up the boxes, dusting, and putting them back down again exactly where they were before. I picked up this one box and it rattled. I don't keep things in boxes, that's not what they're there for. They're there because I like them.

So I opened the box. You'd have done the same, wouldn't you?

Inside was this half a pea size object, hard, or it wouldn't have made a noise in the box, would it? Black and dark green and dark blue then black again, couldn't make up its mind what colour it wanted to be. I tipped it out and let it roll around

147

until it came to a stop and then I looked at it. It was like a large fancy bead except it didn't have any holes in it to thread it onto a cord. I picked it up. It was cold, like ice, and even though I held it for a while it didn't get warm. Not once.

I hadn't seen anything like it.

I showed it to the social services woman who came to see if I needed anything – I said, new lungs, heart, brain, but she didn't smile. No sense of humour, these officials. Stick a laminate on a ribbon, hang it round their neck and all humour goes and all seriousness comes in. Good job I'm not like that, I'd have been in my box a long time back.

She looked at the thing and said she had no idea what it was. Or where it had come from. Or what use it was to anyone.

Well, I thought on that for a while after she went and decided it was no good to anyone. I didn't know what it was, I couldn't use it, I hate keeping things that are no use or not beautiful and believe me, it wasn't beautiful, so I threw it out the window.

Well now, you're going to expect me to say that just like Jack's magic beans, a huge plant grew up overnight and covered the house. Sorry but no. Nothing happened. Nothing at all. It rained a few times, it was sunny a few times, there was a frost and still nothing happened that I could see. My garden, such as it is, looked just the same to me.

How long back was it before the creeping black weed appeared? Two years? More than that? More than that, right. Time slips away when you're elderly and you can't remember from one day to the next which day it is, let alone when you last saw someone. And I can't remember the last time I saw green out there. I miss it; heaven knows how I miss it? Black everywhere. Black trees, leaves, plants, flowers, everything black. Damn weed growing over all paths and roads – I want to know why the scientists can't do anything about it! What is it, do they know?

I know it's alien. Nothing like it has ever been seen on earth before.

Yes, I also know that what I threw out of the window started it.

I'm more sorry than I can tell you about that, but tell me, would you have known it was a seed?

Beauty Sleeps

Bela Lugosi

It is the strangest thing that someone can be the love of your life, the one you cherish beyond all others, the one who holds your very soul in their fine delicate fingers that are like chains, so tight do they hold your priceless gift of love, and yet you look at others.

It is so because I can do nothing else but go with what nature made me – male.

Talk to me not of those who stay devoted to one person their entire married lives, talk to me not of those who fall in love, lose that loved one and never ever look at another person as long as they live.

I disbelieve them.

We are all born with the driving need to perpetuate the species. It is true, this I acknowledge, that men and women have used that excuse for eternity to justify their dalliances outside their relationships which were supposed to be everlasting. It is an excuse. It is also valid.

There are some of us who are driven by darker needs. Those of us who rise and fall with the waxing and waning of the moon phases, those of us who respond to the call of nature in different ways, those whose bodies change and whose physiometry is not entirely under their control. Ah, do you think, even now in this enlightened age, that such mythical creatures as werewolves, vampires, shape-shifters and the like are no more than that, myths? Do you

150

not understand and accept that every myth, no matter how strange, has its basis in fact somewhere in the distant past, even if that past is as distant as the Stone Age and beyond?

Think on it now. Know that dragons once existed as dinosaurs did. Likewise unicorns and werewolves and all the other mythical creatures, mer-people, centaurs, need I go on?

You are asking about the other realms, fairies and the like. They have been with us since the world began; they are timeless, immortal and real. Ask no more. It is fact.

The facts are these.

For the first time in my existence I fell in love.

She was amazing, so beautiful the sun hid its face when she walked the earth.

So intelligent that philosophers stopped their philosophising and listened to her instead.

So joyful that the very birds stopped singing to let her celebrate life.

How trite are these descriptions, how cliché ridden! How truly awful! And yet there is no other way to describe the effect she had on the world – and on me. I was lost. Completely. For the first time I thought I had found someone who would truly hold my love and life for eternity.

In some ways I was right.

In other ways I was not.

We courted, we married, we lived. Within a year I was bored. Beauty at that level is boring as it has no imperfections. Perfection is hard to live with as you constantly measure yourself against it and find yourself lacking. I stared hard at the mirror some mornings and knew, handsome as I know I am, that

I could not match her perfection. When we had dinner parties or entertained in other ways, everyone looked at her and not at me.

The male ego is very easily damaged.

Her knowledge outshone mine. I could not hold an intelligent conversation with her; she would pin down my obvious faults and pour scorn on them.

I looked for others, less beautiful, less intelligent, less knowledgeable. I began to recover my equilibrium.

She suspected, of course.

I denied it, of course.

We continued in a state of truce for a further year when, to my horror, she announced the one thing I had not thought of – she was to have my child.

I should explain that I am not the kind of man who seeks perpetuity through a bloodline. I am not the kind of man who relishes the thought of his home being wrecked with baby items and his sleep wrecked through baby wailing and adoring fluttering people gushing over its every smile, burp and frown.

I took care of that. Knowledge she might have, sense when it comes to the male ego she does not. I took care that she did not discover what had been fed to her and mourned with her at the loss of the child.

But possibly not good enough, for soon after I realised her eyes had turned to another. For a while I encouraged it, the pressure being taken from me, which suited me well but then it galled me that she would look elsewhere.

It was time to take the next step.

The person who supplied the material to induce the miscarriage supplied further material for me.

It worked.

I had her buried, so we had a grave to mourn over and cherish, those of us who professed to love her. I had her buried because I liked the idea of beauty asleep in a grave.

I imagined her rotting, slowly, everything eating her away, slowly.

I played the field, after a due period of mourning had passed, I had fun, something I had forgotten about and could do.

But something was troubling me. Something I felt I had overlooked. Something I should have known – but didn't.

A friend commented that I knew, of course, she was not dead, but sleeping. This is a religious comment and I ignored it. At first. He persisted, telling me over and over that she was not dead but sleeping.

The word 'vampire' was mentioned.

I laughed.

Then I recalled the time I cut myself and she fastened onto the cut and sucked it until I thought she would take the finger clean off my hand.

I wondered why I had been foolish enough not to recognise my own kind.

I had to do something. My mind would not rest.

One dark overcast storm tossed night I took shovel and courage and went to her grave. I dug and dug until I uncovered the coffin, untouched, unscarred by its internment.

When I prised off the coffin lid and looked down at her perfect face, she looked up at me and smiled.

153

Culinary Delights

Charles L Grant

He looked all right on the screen, lived local, quiet life, he said, steady job as some kind of IT consultant – covers a multitude of occupations, that does, if you ask me. He looked all right, pleasant face, smiling eyes, got all his own teeth, what more could someone of my age want in a man?

Would he mind too much that I didn't work, I asked and then answered myself; it didn't matter. He wouldn't get much of a chance to think about that if I played it right.

I had been single and hungry too long. It was time to get out in the Big World and learn how to date, how to do the social small talk, how to charm someone and get what I wanted. Want. Must get it right. You only have one chance at these things, if you don't impress straight off, you blow it.

And I had a need. It had been some time since there was someone in my life, the walls were sick of my conversations and I was sick of the dreary music that kept the neighbours from hearing the conversations with the walls.

Time to play the dating mating game And there he was, on the Singles page, looking for someone just like me, same age, same interests – well, he might think so, for an hour, perhaps, even longer if I could fake it, not bad looking and ready for – whatever it took to snare him. I had to write –

The fingers took over, the brain dictated without the mind being activated, or so it would seem. Before I could stop and think, I had arranged a meeting with Mr. Looks-All-Right-On-Screen.

I had to get the oven cleaned and ready, the table prepared, the knives sharpened and the containers on hand.

I do like my meat to look acceptable on the plate.

I'm tingling with excitement.

It's been a long time since I had long pig.

Autumn Leaves

Edith Wharton

Ellie studied the pattern made by the golden leaves which had drifted from the multitude of twigs and branches on the ancient horse chestnut trees. Ever year Nature created a carpet to walk on, every year the pattern was completely different. Yet no one seemed to notice, no one seemed to appreciate the talent, the artistic flair shown by the different designs.

Autumn leaves. In Autumn everyone leaves. She shivered suddenly as a cold breeze played with her hair and tinged her cheeks with colour. Everyone leaves. In Autumn her father had left, walked out of the door to go to work and never came back. Left them bemused and concerned, then afraid and finally desperately lonely. No police ever came to report a body; no visitor mentioned his not being there. It was as if he had never been. Like Autumn leaves, he had come and gone and few had mourned his passing. Ellie remembered the aching loneliness more than the sorrow, if she had experienced that emotion at all.

Her brother had left in the Autumn, with back pack of books, writing pads, pens, pencils, all the paraphernalia imaginable to study. Virtually no clothes, she recalled, only books and writing things. She had commented on it at the time and had nothing in return but raised eyebrows and a look which said 'don't be stupid.' So she didn't. She let

156

him walk away to University without so much as a hug or a kiss on the cheek or a wish for his future. She had not been on his wavelength at any time during their joint lives, a goodbye would not have made any difference to the way she felt.

They were two then, two people in a house made and furnished for four. Two people who managed to avoid speaking about the things which mattered, the way they felt, the loneliness they endured, the hollow holes in their lives, but instead spoke of late mail delivery, the quality of the food in the local supermarket, the fact that next door were playing their music loud again, even though they had complained. Several times, in fact. Trivial talk. Light talk. As light, as ephemeral as the Autumn leaves which fell, rotted, became one with the earth and enriched it. Their talk would not enrich anything, it added nothing to their lives, to their understanding of life and how to live it, their need to overcome their inhibitions and talk of pain and hurt and suffering and emptiness.

Autumn was an aching time of sadness, melancholia, withdrawal, the windows full of Halloween trivia, as trivial as the talk which sometimes passed for companionship. Autumn was a time of sharp frosts, of rich scents of bonfires, of fruit, the true Harvest Home, the season of richness and of ending. Autumn was a time of dying.

Her mother had died in the Autumn. One day she had sat down in a chair, complained of not feeling well, touched her head theatrically as if in a silent movie melodrama – and stopped breathing. Ellie had, for the longest time, done nothing. She had watched the life empty out of a body and depart and she stood and did nothing. Did not dare to touch the hand, the arm, the shoulder or the face for fear of drawing the life back, for she knew, without being told, that the life had wanted to go, that since her father had walked out of the door and not returned, life had become as melancholy as the season itself, but lasted all year. Only when she grew stiff and her legs ached with standing did she move to the telephone and dial the local surgery, repeating the information to the bored hassled impatient receptionist. Yes, she would wait for the doctor to come. Yes, she would wait for a call. No, it was not a problem.

Only then did she sit down, tucking her feet under the chair, hands in her lap and stared at the person she had called mother but for whom she had no affection whatsoever. Somehow that had dried up, fallen from the branch of family life that was her, drifted to the ground and become compost which, sadly, had produced nothing. At least the Autumn leaves produced fungi and new shoots for wild creatures to sustain themselves. Ellie felt she had been unsustained for many years.

When the men came and took the body away, leaving her with nothing but memories, Ellie blinked a few times, looked around the room and began to catalogue in her mind that which she would keep and that which had to go. There was much to do, so much to do, but she did nothing but look around the room and make her decisions. That would go to the charity shop, that would go to the antique dealer, that would go –

Ellie walked on in the glorious Autumn sunshine, aware of the colours, aware of the brightness of the day, watching other people enjoying the weather, envying the thickness of their padded coats, their boots, their hats and scarves and gloves. Such things she had once and had no longer but the memory of their warmth, their comfort, their sheer – pleasantness, had stayed with her. It was a day for walking and many were doing just that. No one glanced at her as she passed them, absorbed in their own lives, their own words, their own memories.

Ah, that word. Memories. They came with the ability to cut, to hurt, to heal, to please, to fill the heart with joy. There were few of the latter and many of the former. Why was life like that, why was it so hard to find the good in life and so easy to remember the bad? Surely the golden days should stand out, days like today, when the weather was perfect and the carpet freshly laid for all to see and admire?

Everything has to end. Everything has an end. Ellie had reached the end.

She walked and the Autumn leaves were not disturbed by her passing over them.

Road Rage

Richard Laymon

Roads.

Hate them. Damn things just lie there on the ground, stretched out like pieces of black rubber bands or strips cut from tyres and laid there, held down with kerb stones each side or yellow lines or even, heaven forbid, grass because no one goes along there and cuts it, do they? Now why don't I think that a road with a grass edge is a real road?

What does it matter? I still hate them.

Well, listen up and I'll tell you why.

Cos the damn things go *somewhere* and *somewhere* ain't where I wanna go. Not any more, anyway.

Had the wanderlust, I did, itchy feet and all. Remember that silly song 'I was born under a wandering star'? That was me. Wanted to walk the world, I did, see what it looked like in China, Malaysia, Peru, any of them African countries, any of them A-rab countries, wanted to see what made the Arctic different from the Antarctic or were the road signs the same in both places, thick with ice and covered in snow and unreadable...

Joke.

Sorry.

Anyway – got the picture? Wandering me? Left the family a long, long time back, 'cos they didn't want to go wandering, they wanted to sit by the fireside with the dog and the cat and the vegetables in the garden and the thatched roof full of birds and twitters and creepy things that rustled the strands at night and scared the **** out of me. They're welcome to it, I thought, being all of seventeen, all growed up and knowing what I wanted. I thought.

Surprising how wrong you can be, ain't it?

So what I did for a while was, went walking miles and miles, sleeping by roadsides, ear to the ground, hearing the thrum of the lorries, oh man, you could hear them coming for miles, them great wheels pounding the surface and shaking the earth and then going by with a roar and a whooooooosh of wind so sharp and hard it could have you clean off your feet. And gone on to the next village, next town, next city. How come I never stuck out a thumb and got me a ride is the question I am busy asking right now. With no answer, unless it be that I needed to walk it myself, every step, even when dogged tired and feet so sore they could hardly stand the weight of me any more. Talking of that, I lost so much weight I looked like a wraith, or so me Ma said when I went back. Least, I think she said wraith, she might have said rake, come to think on it. Not that it matters, either way I was as thin as one of them reeds thatching our cottage. And come to think on it again, I was fit to rustle like one of them, too, when –

But I ain't there yet.

I'm here. Like here. On the side of the road. Learning to live with the sound of the cars and the lorries and learning which was which, even by the engine and the thrum of the wheels. Oh my, I do like that expression, don't I?

You see, I never learned much in my life up to then, so I set myself the job of learning the difference and it worked and it felt good and I thought – hey, I can do sommat now that perhaps no other person can do! Oh that felt good. I mean, I ain't much good otherwise, am I?

What?

You know that song, "King Of The Road", yes, another song, grew up with songs, could tell you a hundred songs that fit this story, "Road To Hell" is one ... no, that old king of the road song, where he sweeps a floor and things like that. That was me. That was me labouring here and there, fix a gate for someone, muck out the stables for someone else, chop firewood, pluck a chicken, you be surprised how many people want sommat done if you just ask right and don't ask for money. I never did ask for money, never had any either. I got food and a night's shelter and sometimes someone took pity on me and would give me fresh jeans or shirt or a jacket that had a tear here or there but was just fine by me. Oh and a hat to keep the sun off. Suited me just fine.

I did that for what seemed like forever. Enjoyed it no end. Met all sorts of people, learned the good from the bad from the indifferent and the downright mean.

Then I met him.

Hold on. That should be Him.

I was walking this road, see, leaving the lorries and trucks and hauliers to themselves for a while, travelling a back road to see what it felt like. Different, I gotta give you that. Saw a fox or two, all sorts of scurrying things – didn't know what they were, what's the difference between a shrew and a dormouse and a field mouse and a –

Anyway, wild flowers and wild animals and good sunshine and then I realised, in a moment, that someone was walking with me.

There was no one there a breath before, I swear on my reputation, such as it be, as an honest individual. Then he was there. Dark face, dark eyes, dark thoughts and all.

"Do you mind if I share your journey?"

Like he was dressed for it, mind. Sharp suit and white shirt, blue tie crossed with gold lines, smart as you like, complete with polished lace up shoes. Not your usual kit for tramping the road, is it?

But I was brought up proper and even if I had a pretty cute idea of who he was, I said, nice as you like: "You're most welcome."

He hardly seemed to draw breath, was busy talking to me about roads, how they went somewhere and that somewhere was usually more interesting, or so we thought, than the place we had just left, when in truth all places were the same.

"No, they're not," I said when he paused for a moment in his discourse. "The people may look the same, but they ain't."

"Interchangeable, my friend, that's what they are." Then he stopped and looked at me. "You know who I am, don't you?"

"I do."

"And you haven't asked me for anything."

"Why should I? Got all I want outta life."

He frowned. "This isn't right. Everyone wants something."

"I don't."

163

"Not fame, wealth, women?"

Laughter consumed me for a moment. "Fame, me? Got the intelligence of a flea, who's gonna make me famous? Money? Got all I need. Women? You can keep them, nothing but trouble, they be."

"A wise person. I would pick a wise person for today's Good Deed, wouldn't I?"

We were walking again by then, step by step nearer some little town that I had never seen before and would never see again once I passed through, following the road to wherever it led me.

"Well, I suggest you move on and give someone else a Good Deed for the day, sir. I am content with my walking, thank you. Oh, and thank you for your company for this while, too."

His eyebrows went up. "You mean it, don't you? More and more surprising. I cannot go without leaving you a gift, my friend. One that has no strings attached whatsoever. I will make you a telepath. Then you can use the power of your mind to get what you need when you need it, be it food, clothes or shelter."

It sounded good to me, so I said thanks and he – disappeared. I walked on, content.

And then my problems began.

It was a double edged gift indeed. Oh yes, I could use my power to get what I wanted all right, I had food, clothes, shelter aplenty.

I also knew just what those people thought of me. I had their thoughts coming at me, theirs and everyone else's too. It was as if every person was speaking aloud all the time and I could hear everything.

"Here comes a tramp, hide everything afore he steals it."

"Damn cadgers coming in here, wanting sommat for nothing."

"Suppose we'd better give him a job, send him on his way, he can have that meat, it's been off a couple of days but who cares, he'll be long gone by then."

And the other thoughts:

"I hate him, I wish him dead, I hate him and I want him dead..."

"Could throw her down and do it, couldn't I? What could she say, big man like me..."

"Not enough money to buy food, what am I going to do..."

Every thought, every mood, every variation on every human misery there is.

It battered me, it haunted me, it revolted me. You would not believe what thoughts people hide behind smiling faces. Or perhaps you would, if you've been around long enough to know the true heart of man.

I couldn't stand it.

I went back to where I met him, called to him to take his gift back, begged on my knees for my peaceful existence once more – and then I realised what I had done.

I had scorned a gift from the Devil. He had got his own back in such a subtle way that no one could accuse him of being vindictive.

I also realised it wasn't going to go away.

So I braved the town, as it were, got myself some money, bought myself a load of supplies I thought I would need and some I didn't but have sure come in handy and I left the road, climbed up the mountainside and occupied a cave where I live now. The only thoughts I get up there are birds and animals and they don't bother me none.

I venture down occasionally, brave the battering of the townsfolk, buy more supplies, get my beard and my hair cut and get back up out of the way. And there I'll stay until God or the Devil calls me home.

Well now, I better be off. You're thinking you ain't heard such a load of baloney in a long time, right? I see by your face you were disbelieving and now you have to believe 'cos I nailed it, didn't I, everything you were thinking about me.

I'm going back up there, to my cave, where the thoughts are pure and the air is clean and I stay off them roads.

Guess you could call it road rage, of a kind.

Burning Love

Richard Laymon

"How much do you hate him?"

The words seemed to shock the young man. He pushed his tousled hair back with one hand, an obvious time wasting exercise to give him a moment to think before responding. Shock gave way to a glimmer of understanding.

"As much as you."

I laughed, showing him white teeth set amid blood red lips and tongue. No matter his apparent exhaustion, he still twitched. I saw it.

"You can't, my beloved, you can't. I hate him with every fibre of my being and no one can hate more than that."

"Janetta, my darling..." He reached for me but I rolled away, savouring the smell of crushed grass as I did so. Nature at its most basic. Grass crushed beneath a human body.

"Enough, enough! You were wonderful, you are wonderful, my joy, my heart, my life, but no more tonight. I need to think..."

"We've made our plans."

"Randy, you made plans, I am not sure we can go with them just yet."

I rolled over onto my back, gazing up at the velvet night sky, wondering how many stars there were and whether anyone had succeeded in counting them. The thought that each one was a fireball intrigued me, as fire itself intrigued me, the

167

colours, the flickering of the flames, the greed with which it consumed whatever it could find, wood, coal, paper, cloth, flesh, hair, bones...

Those thoughts were best kept very secret indeed. I had Randy where I wanted him, to some degree, but not enough to let him in on my thoughts and dreams and ambitions. Somewhere an owl hooted, close by the undergrowth rustled and I caught sight of a fox loping quietly away, mouth open so it had caught nothing – so far. Well, that makes two of us, my friend, I mused and laughed silently.

"I'm getting cold." Randy got up and began swinging his arms around to generate some heat. Reluctantly I got up, without his help. Lithe and sinuous as I am, I could get myself up from the ground without assistance. It was something he said he admired, my independence, which translated to my inability to accept help. I thought it was a drawback; there were times when a little help would not come amiss.

"I'm going home," I announced with an edge on my voice that said 'no argument.' Randy nodded, a movement I could just about see in the darkness caused by the huge oak.

"Then let's go."

We walked along the edge of the cornfield, the ears ripe and ready for harvest, the wind stirring them so they spoke in sibilant whispers to one another. I wondered if anyone could speak the language of the corn and if they could, what they would learn. Then I berated myself for stupid thoughts. Hold on to reality, I told myself. There is one big thing to do and the sooner you do it, the better.

Randy left me at the steps leading up to the house. He walked off without once looking back, just as I had told him to do, so why the tinge of disappointment that he hadn't turned round once to look at me? What good was a lover if they didn't act like one? Even if it meant breaking the rules I had given him ... but then, had I not chosen him because he was compliant, meek and obedient?

I hurried up the steps, my footfall silent in expensive leather pumps. The door eased open without a sound and I slipped through the gap, all but holding my breath. There was no member of staff around that I could see. With a sigh of relief I climbed the stairs to my room, where I locked the door behind me and threw myself on the bed, only then realising I had been actually been holding my breath all the way up.

Hate.

An all consuming emotion that blinds people to reality, reasonable thought, often reasonable behaviour. Hate. Hatred. Loathing. Detestation. Whatever the name, whatever the word, the object of that hate became unbearable.

And Stuart Edward Philip De Vere Walston, my husband of ten years and three days, if I was counting – which I surely was – had become unbearable to my vision, my hearing and my touch. His voice grated on me, his platitudes were a patronising condescension – if I could phrase it thus – and all I wanted, dreamed of, visualised over and over, was plunging a sharpened steak knife into his starched shirt front, seeing the richness spill out and stain the white and then the black of his ubiquitous evening suit. The problem: that vision was swiftly accompanied by the one of the police arriving, arresting me and taking me away in handcuffs, incarcerating me in some ghastly prison cell for years and years.

Even hate has a price, a step it is impossible to take for the sake of sanity.

Oh, but there are other ways to wreak revenge.

I sat up, reached for a cigarette and then remembered I had quit smoking a week earlier. No, that was the wrong term; I had decided to delay having a cigarette. The 'delay' had now gone on for just over a week and it was getting easier, although I missed the feel of the slender tobacco packed tube in my fingers, the flare of the lighter, the flame which brought instant relaxation and pleasure. Ignore the ash, the tainted breath, the smelly clothes, the tarred lungs...

Stop it, I told herself. Stop it! Anyone can do diversionary tactics like that.

Face facts.

My husband, the local squire, land owner, Master of the Hunt, benefactor to the local community, is a two timing nasty piece of work.

Under the clothes, no one can see the bruises from the vicious pinches or sly jabs with an elbow, hard enough to damage.

He thinks I don't know about his dalliances, his one night stands, his longer term affairs, thinks I can't see the looks he gives to the current one who has caught his attention, someone who will be bought off when he's bored, in about three weeks, judging by the rate he gets through them.

And I get Randy, a farm hand, a rough and ready labourer. The thing is, Randy is always ready and if he is sometimes rough, it doesn't matter.

Randy professes to hate my husband as much as I do. I disbelieve him for his home, where he and his older brother still live, is owned by the farm and by my husband. His job is dependent on my husband. He can tell me he hates him but I disbelieve him and know that apart from me, no one hates him for no one sees him as I do. But he's useful, he's discreet, he's young, he has staying power and he's good looking. And in awe of me. What more could I ask?

Well, peace of mind for one.

How to get it is something else.

I am not letting my husband continue to get away with endless affairs, which he flaunts in front of me, knowing well that I am aware of them. Is it my fault he scorns my room and my bed? Is it my fault I am no longer the young woman he courted and married? Does it not occur to him that he too is ten years older and sagging in places?

I know what I want to do. I know it well enough that I can see it happening and, with the right circumstances, no one will know anything about it until it is over. None of this hacking at his chest with a steak knife and having witnesses to the act. No, nothing as crude as that.

Hit him where it hurts. In the bank account.

All I have to do is work out the very best way of doing it...

I was the model wife for some weeks. Entertaining guests, running the house, supervising

171

the perfect meals, I did nothing that he could criticise in any way, shape or form. He did not visit my room, for which I was grateful, for I would have found it difficult to respond with enough ardour to satisfy him. That I saved for Randy and nights on the edge of the cornfield, with the rustling sound of the corn talking to itself as background to my cries of passion.

It was then the seed of an idea came to me.

The first task was to find out where my husband conducted his dalliances with his latest paramour. Slut, whore, two timing friend ... the names could go on forever but were futile, he had power, money and status, she had ambitions and that I understood. My revenge was not going to be against someone he had managed to entrap, but against him, the monster, the ogre, the bane of my days and my existence.

I bribed a stable lad to follow them one night, to find out where they went when she visited our estate. Simple, he said, they were so engrossed in one another they had no idea he was following. They went to a small cottage on the outskirts of the land, one I had seen many times when out riding but ignored. It was tumbledown, in drastic need of renovation and repair and I never thought about why recently the roof had been patched, the windows replaced, the door shutting properly. Foolish woman that I am, I thought perhaps he planned to put a tenant in there. Instead he was using it to put a part of him into her. I wondered what it was like inside the cottage, how much effort he had made, without actually wanting to find out.

Mixed up feelings fighting for precedence and none of them winning.

He spoke at dinner about the money we would reap – I use the word advisedly – when the harvest was gathered in, mentioned the high price of corn, the heavy crop we had raised this year together with the barley and the wheat. He spoke of a new carriage, we could afford it, he said, when it was sold and the money banked safely. I sat and listened and nodded and said 'yes' in the right places and smiled at him as if delighted with the fact we could have a new carriage and money in the bank, as if that made up for his philandering right before my eyes. I saw nothing but my need for revenge. I ask now, do you blame me? Have not countless women – and men, come to that – felt the same over the centuries, when they find the love of their life has been dallying with someone else? My problem was, he was not the love of my life in the first place, but he was *my* husband, the fact I didn't care about him was immaterial. Possession is everything. He chose me before he chose them. Illogical I know, but to me it was perfect feminine reasoning.

I chose a night when Randy was full on ready in every sense of the word. We met at our trysting place, the base of the oak, where undergrowth had created its own enclosure. We met and we loved intensely for some time. Then I complained I really needed a cigarette and pulled the box of matches from my pocket. Randy laughed; he had never seen me smoke and could not believe I did, or that I owned such things. I had a cigarette with me but had no intention of lighting it. Instead I struck the match, missed the cigarette, to his amusement, and

173

threw the lighted match onto the patch of fuel I had quietly placed in the corn an hour or so before we met.

It was spectacular. An entire cornfield went up in flames in no time at all, the corn no longer whispered, it shrieked in its dying throes. At least, that is what I heard, the dying of the corn. I could almost hear my husband shrieking at the loss of income from the harvest.

It was only when the flames had died down that the source of the shrieks was discovered. Instead of using the cottage that night, he and his paramour had chosen a place in the corn.

I had my witness in Randy who swore that I had thrown a match away that I shook to extinguish the flame before I threw it. I had the staff who spoke of my husband's dalliances with all and sundry and how he normally used the cottage but this night had seemingly changed his mind.

Revenge is a dish best served cold? No, revenge comes in flickering flames, intense heat and the sure knowledge that the memories will live with you forever.

I ask you, how many women get to burn down a cornfield – and their cheating husband with it?

The corn has grown again and it whispers its secrets. I am grateful now that no one understands the language that it speaks.

Countdown To Death

Antony Woodville

It never fails to surprise me how quickly a beautiful day can turn into a black one without a hint of warning. When a storm approaches, the air changes and there are warnings. On the beautiful April day of which I am thinking there was no warning. I was walking in Ludlow Castle grounds with Edward, Prince of Wales when the gates were flung open and an exhausted lathered horse carrying an equally exhausted rider came into the courtyard. Stable hands rushed to take the horse and the rider, wearing Edward IV's emblem, staggered wearily over to kneel at my feet. Or so I thought. In truth, he was kneeling at the feet of young Edward. He looked up at the boy and said, 'Your Grace, I bring you sad news. Your father died of a tertian fever two days ago.'

We were all shocked but even as I stood there assimilating the tragic news, I noticed that young Edward had taken the news calmly, as if he had expected it, whilst I myself went cold from head to foot. It is a trite expression to say 'life would never be the same again' but in this instance it carried more truth than it would normally. The passing of a King means dramatic and often traumatic changes; I wondered just what life would bring us.

I gave orders that the messenger be taken care of, he had ridden hard and long to get to us and it showed. And then I turned and knelt before the new

King to offer him my fealty. With perfect dignity and aplomb, he held out his hand and said, 'Uncle Rivers, please get up. I will have need of you in the days ahead and would wish that we could be on the same terms as we were before we had this news.' The intention was good, but our roles had changed. I was no longer the guardian and tutor of the Prince of Wales; I was now employed by Edward V.

It was at this point that the new King burst into tears, which I was mighty glad to see as I was beginning to think he had not a natural bone in his body.

For a time life became surreal, there was so much to do. The new King had to be conveyed to London in style, which meant a large retinue of armed men and a revamp of his wardrobe, because he would be in deep mourning. The whole Castle was in uproar as plans were made, discarded, new plans made, amended and in the middle of all this an effort to keep Edward relatively calm and comforted, for we had not to lose sight of the fact that whereas we had lost a King, Edward had lost a father. He might have been a distant figure, there were many miles between us, but the fact remained that his mother was a good distance away, at a time when he could have done with her comfort, of that I am sure.

I offer this as my explanation, my rationalisation, for not taking into account the influence of Richard of Gloucester, the King's brother and possibly his most loyal subject. It was something I would later regret.

Somehow, by what alchemy I do not now recall, we organised the journey to London. A large retinue of men, some six hundred of them, supply wagons, fresh horses, squires and servants rode out from Ludlow Castle, with the new king, his attendants, I and my attendants at the head of the procession. We all wore deep mourning and with pennants flying and arms flashing in the sunlight, we must have made an impressive sight. Overall there was a sense of jubilation tempered by sadness, a strange mixture, but who could take from the boy the fact he had become King overnight and was being accorded all the respect that the new title brought him. It had to be an exciting time. He rode a pure white horse which contrasted dramatically with his black clothes. I thought he cut a fine figure and, for a moment, envied him his youth and the life he had ahead of him.

The noise was quite overwhelming, the jingle of harness, the many hooves striking the earth, the creaking of the supply carts, the screaming chatter of the birds which circled overhead as if giving us their benediction for the journey – or were they issuing a warning? I looked up with distaste; I have never cared for crows. They feed on carrion. I could have done without their farewell chorus. Some things are beyond our capability to control, the sight and sound of birds is just one of them.

Had I known then I would never ride through Ludlow's great gate again, I would have taken the time to look back at the sturdy walls and soaring towers of one of my favourite places. But the day was bright, the company was relatively cheerful, Edward himself was excited at going to London after being in Ludlow for some time, quite apart from his new role and I had no reason to believe I would not return one day to my chambers, where so much of my wardrobe was held, where a good many of my books together with my possessions resided.

Sunshine and a sense of excitement. There was chatter between us all, talk of the journey, of the future, of what Edward would do when he got to London, all this created a good feeling, despite the fact we were in mourning for a king and so there was no reason for the cold feeling that swept over me when we were about halfway to a place called Stony Stratford. We planned a halt there – ah, with hindsight I realise just what those words meant - and as the day progressed everyone became quieter and more tired.

There were so many of us we decided to divide into two groups for the night, Edward and his attendants, together with half the armed men, were to go to Northampton whilst I, with the remainder of the men, rode into Stony Stratford, still wondering why I felt the chill of premonition, asking myself what I could do about it – if anything.

Too late. Richard of Gloucester was there with the smiling false-faced Buckingham at his side. We greeted one another cordially enough. I recall admiring Gloucester's new mourning outfit; even his jewellery was the most intense black imaginable. That was for show, his inner feelings were revealed by the dark rings under his eyes and the lines of suffering carved into a face which did not smile often at the best of times. He seemed to me to be fighting hard to keep his emotions under control. He offered me a sort of smile, thin enough to slice meat, I thought, and invited me to dinner with him. I agreed, knowing in my heart that I had no alternative, that from there onwards my fate was not in my hands but his. It never was again.

There was no spectre at the meal, we ate, drank, talked, exchanged anecdotal stories of Edward and his great appetite for food, wine and women and even laughed occasionally. Buckingham had an endless source of stories, some of which I knew, some were new but not exactly fit for the company in which he found himself, a brother and a close friend both bereaved but he was ever thoughtless and did not seem to realise he was being crass.

When I knew my limit for wine had been reached I made my excuses, offered my thanks and went to the room allocated to me. And laid awake wondering what was ahead, for I knew, with absolute surety, the two of them were scheming something. I recalled the flash in Gloucester's eyes when he casually said 'my brother appears to have made me Lord Protector, so his son is now my charge.' That was like a blow to the stomach. I had cared for and tutored the boy for some time, I thought of him as my son, having none of my own on whom to lavish love and attention. That comment said 'from now on he is mine.'

In the darkness of that long night – and it seemed as if it lasted twice as long as any normal night I had known – I relived my times with the deceased Edward, recalled the good times along with the bad, mourned for my sister and their brood of children and, selfishly, for myself for I had every reason to believe my life was over and done.

The morning proved me right.

I looked out of the grimy window to see that the inn was surrounded by a ring of armed guards wearing Gloucester's insignia. Mine had been dismissed, it would seem. I dressed and went down for breakfast, where I was formally placed under arrest for treason. I could almost believe Gloucester was smiling behind the mask of rigidity he displayed as his men led me away. Perhaps I felt it more than saw it. I know not whether the man was at all psychic or even sensitive to others, but I was and I knew well that he was gloating inside. For all his apparent indifference, he disliked the Wydevilles. The placement of carts full of arms, bearing the Wydeville arms, had been interpreted as treason, as if we knew Edward was going to die so suddenly, that Gloucester had been appointed Lord Protector, as if we had done more than follow Edward's paranoid orders and put the arms ready in the event of an attack from the North, despite his brother being in control in that area. Who knew what went on in Edward's often wine befuddled mind toward the end, or indeed what truly went on behind Gloucester's implacable mask? What I read, in the brief moments when he spoke with me before I was hustled away, was 'at last I have the Wydevilles where I want them!' I recall not the words, only the feelings. They were and are more reliable than any utterances

Sheriff Hutton castle is not the most comfortable of dwellings. I had been in many castles, Warwick had offered me accommodation at his homes in the past, but nothing prepared me for the barrenness of this place. Bare walls, floors without coverings, bed without hangings, chairs with minimal padding, it seemed more a prison than anything. I could not think it to be anything but.

Thomas Vaughan had been arrested and hapless Richard Grey, my nephew, all of nineteen years of age with a life ahead of him, were also held, so I was told.

None shared my prison cell. No living person shared my prison cell. But oh the shades which came to talk, to commiserate, to console! My father and brother came, victims of Warwick after the shambles of Edgecote, my two dead brothers came, those who preceded me and did not live to see childhood, my mother, now smiling having been reunited with her beloved and the one I sought most, the one I longed for most, she of the laughing eyes, tumbled mass of hair and body that delighted until the canker ate her from the inside and reduced her to a living skeleton, my adored and loved Elizabeth. I wrote dutifully to my wife, my current wife, but there was not the feeling in the letters there should be, for she had not been anything like a replacement, nor had I intended her to be. There had been but one love for me and she I lost to the Reaper far earlier than I wanted. If there was consolation at all in the knowing the day would come when my head would be separated from my body, it was in her presence and she, more than the others, lingered by my side and filled my room with light. My father bid me have courage, my mother mourned I would not live on and told me she feared for my sister's sanity, as if I could do aught about it for her. Elizabeth just said it would not be long and we would be reunited. In that I found acceptance and peace at the prospect of death.

I was busy at first, sending letters to my business agent to settle my affairs, drafting a will and wondering who to ask to prove it for me, writing to my wife to ensure her future was settled too. Then ennui set in and it was then I spent long hours talking with Elizabeth. It was her suggestion I ask the so-called Lord Protector – I never did see the document which appointed him to the position and I knew I never would – as it would go down well and possibly help my sister. I hated the thought but knew she made sense.

But for all my need to be reunited with my beloved wife, I really did not want to die. I had delivered a second book to William Caxton; I longed to see it printed and hold a copy in my hands, as I had with my first book. I longed to see Middleton Hall again and Caister and all the other homes I had as part of my estates. I longed to go to the Island and stay at Carisbrooke Castle, to see the ending of the work of building the towers at the entrance, all work I had set in hand and had to leave to my brother Edward to continue for me. He promised he would but that was not the same as seeing the finished work myself. It never would be. I found myself mourning that as well. I loved the castle there, I loved the island. I would never see any of it again.

Elizabeth hushed me when I spoke thus, telling me it mattered not, that I could travel there once I was free of my earthly body and free of Gloucester and his wiles and – dare I say it? jealous deceits.

There, it is said and I have at last expressed my feelings.

I watched the days go by, the rain, the wind, the sunshine. Watched and counted. 56 days of solitude and emptiness, of waiting for the summons for I knew I would be called and I was, eventually. The night before I was bid to leave Sheriff Hutton I spent time mulling over a ballad which quite amused me for a time. At least I would leave that for posterity, if naught else. Ah, but my book was there and always would be there, Elizabeth reminded me, with her radiant smile. None could take that from me, no matter what.

By morning they had come for me. Destination, Pontefract Castle, they told me. Why, I had no idea. I did not ask. By then there was nothing in my head but longing for it to be over – there is just so long you can be the courageous aristocrat, just so long you can hold on without wanting to break down completely and beg for clemency and look a fool doing it. Not that it would be granted anyway.

Pontefract was sunshine and avid onlookers, well, Gloucester's men anyway. Richard was holding it together, just, Thomas was stern faced and resigned. Ratcliffe, I refuse to give him his title, Gloucester's axeman in every sense of the word, asked for last words, as if we had been through a formal trial. No one answered him.

Richard, with a bravery I admired, walked over to the block and knelt down. I felt my heart break as his head was severed and his body thrown to one side. Ratcliffe beckoned to me and I turned just once to smile at my beloved, walking by my side. *Hold on,* she whispered, *it will soon be over.*

It was. In the final seconds when I knelt and waited, I wondered what they would make of the hair shirt I wore under my finest doublet. That would give them cause to think for a moment or two of the man they had removed from life.

Then it was done.

Given under the seal of Antony Wydeville, Lord Scales of Newcelles and the Isle of Wight, 2nd Earl Rivers this day in March 2011.

Note by Antony Woodville:

The date of my execution was the 25th June 1483. My channel, she who was my beloved Elizabeth, uses a contraction of that date as her email address. In some places on the Internet she is known as Antonia Woodville. Through her the Wydevilles live on. She fights for our reputation and our name. One day, when she is sufficiently well known for her historical writing, she is going to search for my bones and I will, at last, have a proper funeral and resting place. Only she knows what that will mean to me.

Life Changes

Richard Laymon

The parking meter said there was still one hour of parking time left.

The shame was the driver had gone, taking their ticket with them. One hour wasted. But the parking space was available, can't have everything in this life. Slide the car into the slot, pay for a ticket and drop it on the dash for the ever intrusive traffic wardens to see, lock the door and go.

To what?

Why had he asked for the meeting? And in such a public place? Franco's, for goodness' sake! Packed to the doors usually with avid diners, as in avid eaters and listeners. It did not bode well for the future of our relationship.

He said in his voicemail, 'don't book longer than an hour; no need to give them money unnecessarily.' But dinner at Franco's took two hours, start to finish, lingering over liquors afterwards and all.

To what? The question came up again in my mind.

The end, of course. Why else invite me to a one hour meeting in our favourite restaurant where we always spend two hours... why speculate? Heels clicking, I headed for Franco's, trying to quell the butterflies and sickness churning in my stomach. Whoever said there was such a thing as heartache was wrong. It's stomach ache - every time.

Cold, bitterly cold. The wind played with litter, tossing it here and there, occasionally getting bored and throwing a hat into the game instead until it was rescued by its irate owner. Boot heels clicked on the chilled pavement, eyes seeking the warmth were attracted by steamed up windows which said 'in here is hot, hot, hot!' but they weren't Franco's and the man I loved would not be there, waiting.

Fingertips began to ache with the cold. Come on, hurry, would that I could have found a parking place nearer!

At last, the door opened into warmth, rich smells of good food and richer coffee, ears assaulted with clink of cutlery on china and the rolling massed sound of voices.

He sat alone at a table for two, frowning. I knew that frown so well, it boded ill for the meeting.

I waved, he looked up and smiled. Franco's waiter took my coat, I made my way through the tables and chairs to the chair opposite him and sat down.

'What...'

His gesture said silence. The waiter came; I ordered a starter and a large coffee. I saw he had nothing in front of him. The water went away without asking him what he wanted. The cold which I had walked in had come in to the restaurant with me; it sat low and angry and grew infinitesimally as we looked at one another across the clarity of the white tablecloth.

'Don't be angry.' His voice was low, laden with unbearable sadness and then I knew. Knew with absolute certainty that our time together was done.

The coffee came, steaming, tempting, cream floating swirling on the top, even as my emotions were swirling as I tried to come to terms with the ending of something wonderful.

'How long have you known?'

'Ah, you would ask that, my loved one. Three days. I have been thinking on our past for three days now and cried a million tears. I'm all cried out.' But he wasn't, a stray tear was creeping down his face and he dashed it away with a hand that was quickly restored out of sight under the table.

Not before I saw it. The hair was long, dark and thick.

It had begun.

It was over.

I drank the coffee, holding the cup in both hands, staring into the darkness of its depths. He said nothing, waited as I thought about everything and absorbed it.

'It's been good.'

'I hoped you would say that.'

'It has been more than good, it has been wonderful. I will be a long time finding another like you.'

He laughed gently. 'I hope not exactly like me, or you will have to go through this again.'

'If all of your type are like you, then I would face it and handle it and love him as I have loved you.'

'Thank you.' Another tear. It had been an outrageous lie that they were done.

I had no tears. They would come later.

'Now I understand why you told me only to pay for an hour. You've shut down, you're not eating

187

and I could not sit here and eat a meal while you had nothing.'

'Precisely.'

The cold had gone. In its place was aching grief, loss and pending loneliness. A different feeling entirely. Why had I been so certain he was dumping me? Foolish, foolish person that I am. I should have known his love was greater than that.

I did not expect this so soon. He said we had some years ahead of us. Maybe he miscalculated. I dared not ask.

'How much...'

'A lot. This is the last time I can come out in public.'

The starter came, I prodded at it, ate a few mouthfuls, pushed it away. It was good but my appetite had gone.

'Your hour is going fast.'

'It means nothing if this is our last hour together.'

'I would not have you leave knowing there was a parking ticket waiting for you!'

The laugh I loved, low, sexy and inviting, was still there. Everything was still there, it was just that it would be smothered under layers of thick dark hair very soon, the face would change, a muzzle would form, the arms would change and lengthen, the spine curve, a long tail would emerge and the man I loved would become a wolf. A werewolf.

I knew that werewolves could be human for a long, long time, changing now and then but that the time would come when the change was permanent. He had told me, freely so I knew what I was getting into, that this was his last time. When he changed back, he would not be able to be human again.

I thought I could handle it.

I found I couldn't.

I had dreaded this day from the moment we fell in love. Now it was here.

I got up, fumbled for money but he pushed it away. 'My treat. Go enjoy your life. It's been – wonderful. Better than any before. Hold on to that.'

I nodded and walked over to the door. The waiter handed me my coat, sympathy radiating out of him. He knew. Somehow he knew and he had not questioned anything. I thanked him as best I could and hurried out into the coldness.

The wind brought tears to my eyes; it was the wind, yes?

But not enough tears that I couldn't see the parking ticket stuck on my windscreen when I got there. I had gone over the hour after all.

Just as I had gone over the time with the werewolf who had stolen my heart.

Unless I could find another – and what were the chances of that happening? I was going to be lonely for a very long time.

The trouble was, I needed to find another. Who else understood the need to take time out every full moon and hide? The other trouble was, I had a long way to go before I could change back and stay that way forever.

I knew when I did, I would seek him out and we would for eternity.

Before then there was a life to lead. It did not involve paying for time.

I tore off the parking ticket and went to find the traffic warden. It was close enough to full moon for me to have begun the change.

Some people should be careful whose car they target...

The Pied Piper's Story

Roald Dahl

It was a fairly stylish town, as they go, beautiful buildings, soaring churches, elegant homes, wide spacious streets and a town council that was doing no more than looking out for itself.

Pompous they were, the councillors, in expensive suits and silk shirts, elaborate ties, highly polished shoes. Oh I must mention the carefully barbered hair, the manicured nails, the air of affluence they carried with them. It was as strong as perfume.

Those well fed faces were adorned with worry lines when I got there. It had been a long time since I had seen people that concerned, so I knew there was a major problem going on. I smiled, I laughed, I talked lightly, but beneath it all they knew there was a hint of steel. They knew I was not to be messed with. So I ask you in all honesty, why did they do it?

But let me go back to the beginning. The grapevine is by far the most reliable way of getting information. You can forget writing letters, sending messengers, anything that involves an additional way of getting news to someone, just let the gossip do the work for you. This is what happened. I was some miles away from the town when I started to hear rumours of a problem. It had to be a problem that I could resolve, provided the money was right. I am not that foolish that I work for nothing. Well, would you?

191

I set out to walk to the town, reasoning that the longer I took to get there, the greater the problem would be and therefore the more pleased they would be to see me. You see, I have done this before. Quite a few times, in fact.

It was a beautiful summer's day when I set out. Walking in the sunshine is not a trial to me, I have a ready enough smile and sufficiently charming manner to ensure I get fed and watered along the way. Sure enough, cottagers offered me milk, bread, fresh churned butter, rich cheese, fine hams, even fresh cooked chicken at one point. I ate well; I slept on thick straw and once even on a thick mattress. I have to say my journey was good. I was almost unhappy that I finally arrived at my destination.

But not too much, for I could almost see the gold coins before my eyes, having walked into the town and seen the problem.

I sat in the town square for a little while, letting the people see me, letting them gossip about me, knowing that it would get back to the councillors very quickly. It did. Again, this is something I have done many times in many places. The Mayor bustled out to see me, seemingly in a hurry, but he had stopped long enough to don his gold chain. It was as if he had to have his badge of office before he had the confidence to come and speak with me. I wonder if I really am that scary. Or was it an act for the benefit of the councillors?

By the time he arrived I had been sitting there for about half an hour. Long enough to have seen at least thirty rats scampering here and there, stealing food, copulating, doing everything that rats do but here they were bolder, more obvious, than anywhere

I had been before. The town was over-run with them.

"Sir..." The Mayor was uncertain of how to approach me. What did I look like to him, I wondered? Sometimes I had no control over the way I looked. I thought I was representing myself as a smart businessman, but – on second thoughts, having walked there, how could I?

For a fleeting moment I stood outside myself and looked at the figure sitting on the bench. Oh my, no wonder he did not know what to do or say: damn fool outfit of many colours, bell on my hat – where in the name of Hell did that lot come from? Did my Master have such a distorted sense of humour?

Back in my body I gave the Mayor my best smile and stood up. "Sir," I said in return, "you have a problem here, rats!"

"I know." He looked relieved and then worried again. "Can you help?"

"I can. The question is, will I? What is your offer to rid the town of rats?"

"Ten gold coins."Another councillor pushed forward, eager, polished face and polished manner. I distrusted him instantly.

"Fifteen."

The Mayor turned slightly green just as another rat darted out of the baker's opposite us. "Are you confident you can rid us of the vermin?" he asked, almost through gritted teeth.

"I am."

"Who are you?" asked another councillor, narrow of face and narrow of vision.

I recalled my strange outfit and smiled again. "They call me the Pied Piper, sir."

I put just enough emphasis on the 'sir' to remind him he had not given me the courtesy of a title. Sure enough he blushed and stood back. Now let me say this: the money was of no consequence, I could not take it back with me. The point was, the townspeople had to want me to do the job or I couldn't do it. That meant paying the price I asked, even if it hurt.

"All right." The Mayor finally gave in. "You dispose of the rats and we will give you fifteen gold coins."

I think I knew at that point they would try and get out of it.

The whistle was my chosen 'weapon', it worked every time, whether a town wanted to be rid of rats, crows, mice, or any other plague that was bothering them. It was a fun thing to do, for me, and a surprising amount tried to renege on the agreement, which gave me more scope for malicious fun. Fools. They had no idea who they were dealing with.

I walked around the town playing a tuneful little ditty that the rats could not resist. They came running; they came so fast they snatched up their babies from the nests and brought them along too. Before long there was a heaving river of brown rats flowing through the town. I lengthened my stride and led them to the nearby river, changing the tune at the end so the whole lot ran into the water and drowned.

I went back to the town square and sat on the bench where I had been earlier. Suddenly there was no one there. Not a single resident. The Mayor was no doubt locked in his office, putting his gold chain back in its box after being carefully polished and cleaned and leered over.

No one came with money. Hamelin was devoid of rats and people. I was devoid of payment and people to speak to. I was no longer wanted.

Just what I knew was going to happen.

I knew just what to do, too.

I began another tour of the town, playing a different tune this time, a lively little dance number. One by one the children came from their rooms, their gardens, their play areas, they came and they danced along behind me. I heard parents calling wildly to their offspring to come back but I had them entranced. I heard the Mayor bellowing after me for forgiveness, but by then I was halfway out of the town and heading for the countryside. I ignored him. He had one chance and he blew it.

The mountain was relatively close, not in human terms but close enough for those of us with devilish superhuman powers. I transported the whole lot of them to the mountain, opened a door and allowed them all to go in. Then I slammed the door...

I walked back into Hamelin and there they all were; parents, councillors, Mayor. He who had questioned me was bright red with fury but dared do nothing, especially when he saw first my wings, indicating I was an angel and then the horns, which indicated I was a dark angel. Then he cowered in his suit and his fury turned to fear. As it had to.

"You cheated me." I spoke in a normal voice but my anger showed and they all took several steps back. "Now I have cheated you. I ask you, is it fair to render nothing for services rendered?" I did like that turn of phrase, I had been practising it for many a long year. And used it many times too.

They were silent.

"Sir?" The voice was small, the voice of a child. I turned and saw a crippled boy on his crutches looking up at me. "Sir, will you take me to the mountain and reunite me with my playmates, please?"

"No!" shrieked an anxious looking woman, clutching at the boy's arm. He pulled away.

"I don't want to live here without any children," he explained.

Was I in the mood for a good deed? Not really but would it do any harm? Would my Master be offended if I did such a thing? I doubt he would worry unduly. I made up my mind in that moment.

"Of course. Come with me."

I scooped him up and we flew to the mountain, where I opened the door and let him go in.

Then I closed the door again.

And I left Hamelin forever.

Well, that's what happened and that's where the legend arose about the strange man who took the rats and the children away from the town.

What they don't know, those who tell the tale over and over, is that I have a problem.

Those damn kids.

They follow me everywhere.

And for that, my Master is not best pleased. He told me to return them but none wanted to go back. My life is more interesting than the one they had in Hamelin, now they get to go places by utilising my energy and – I have to admit – draining me so I cannot always fly.

Heaven must be laughing at me.
Hell certainly is.

Gabriel's Revenge

Gabriel

You don't mess with Gabriel.

All right, it's a pretty banal thing to say in some respects, but in others ... I mean, a benevolent Archangel, right? Sitting at the feet of God, right? Overseeing all the angels and cherubim and seraphim and the like, right?

Wrong.

Gabriel is God's watchman, taskmaster, overseer, supervisor and all the other titles you can think of. He doesn't sit for a moment, never takes the weight off his weary legs and wings. Talking of which, he hates the things, don'tcha know ... moans about them constantly, how they get in the way when he goes through doorways and how they bother him when he does get a second to sit – which is probably why he doesn't.

On the other hand, how would he get around Heaven so fast if he couldn't fly? He's smart but teleporting himself, he hasn't got that far yet. One day he will, I swear it. There ain't nothing that Archangel can't do – or know.

And that's where the problem lies.

Ha! What a choice of word there, lies. 'Twas that which brought me down here, if you get my drift.

You see, well, perhaps you don't but let's go through it from sad start to sorry finish and see what sense we make of it.

Gabriel's got a lot of people he's supposed to be looking after – and I do mean a lot. Not quite half the population of earth but you get the message ... well, perhaps that's a small exaggeration – all right, a big one. What did I say about lies? You don't believe everything that comes out of a demon's mouth, do you? You do? Mad fool.

All right ... Gabriel has a few people he is especially in charge of and one he seems excessively fond of. I don't get it; mostly I don't like humans very much. Oh, I kept this to myself in the Heavenly Realms, down here I get to shout it to the rooftops (if we had any) if I want.

I DON'T LIKE HUMAN BEINGS!

There, I said it. Good and loud.

I didn't think Archangels were allowed favourites, but then, being Archangels, I suppose they can do just what they like, no questions asked, no need for answers. Or lies.

Not that an Archangel would lie, they don't know the meaning of the word.

Anyway ... damn, do I keep going off topic, or what? Never make a writer, would I?

There I am, deputising for Himself cos he's off gallivanting around the Realms seeing to this and seeing to that and I am supposed to stop this person, this female, from damaging herself or doing anything which stops her doing what she's supposed to do, get on with the spirit work we've (they've) given her to do.

And guess what the silly ***** does? Goes and hurts herself when I wasn't looking.

Now, I told Gabriel that I was looking but I didn't move quick enough to stop her pick up the box of books, turn sideways and do herself a near fatal injury.

Truth is, I wasn't looking and didn't know a thing about it until the next morning when she's rolling around the floor in agony with a strangulated hernia and it's off to hospital and a life saving operation and the whole carnival show.

And Gabriel, disbelieving Archangel that he is, winds time back twenty four hours and sees me skiving off watching some girly show on the beach instead of watching his special one.

Damn. I had forgotten he could do that.

The row that went on! The shouting and stamping and wing clashing that went on you would not believe. Nothing like it on Earth, so I can't give you the equivalent scenario, you just gotta imagine an irate Archangel, with huge wings and huge temper, letting loose on a poor little angel-turned-demon who just took some time out to go do a normal thing, watch the girly show and not his girl. How was I to know she would be that stupid?

Well, I know that was what I was there for ... to get between her and the box and stop her doing it. And I didn't.

You mess with an Archangel - you get thrown out.

And I was, immediately. No chance to pack, so my robe, my books, my music and my cherished harp are still there, in a box, probably with my name still on it. I won't get it back, ever.

It doesn't matter one whit.

I'm having more fun here.

The girls are real down here, hot, hot and ready for more heat too, if they can stand it, so can I. No one watching over me and no one for me to watch over. Get up when I want, go to bed when I want, do what I want with who I want to do it with.

Who needs the Heavenly Realms?

I don't!

I'm lying again, aren't I?

I want to go back. I want to be with the other angels and cherubims and seraphims and make my obeisance to God now and then and say Hi to Michael, Raphael and Uriel and the other Archangels. And hang out with Gabriel now and then, 'cos he really is fun to be around.

Even if it means watching over his loved one again.

Damn it to heaven, I want to go back.

And I can't.

Now I'm finding out what hell is really like.

And it isn't much fun.

I Will Wait For You

Richard Laymon

The City of London, ancient as the ground it
stands on, modern as the towering strange buildings
it has seemingly manufactured out of nothing, has
more than its share of graveyards.

The worker and casual visitor to the Square Mile,
where money changes hands at an alarming rate,
where fortunes are made and lost, where the Bank
of England sits like the old lady she has been
likened to and holds on to the riches she has
acquired over the countless years of being in the
centre of the Square Mile of commerce, are not
always aware of them.

Most cities never sleep, but this one does. This
one closes down at night, leaving the rats and strays
to haunt the narrow alleyways, the wide affluent
streets, the banks of the great never sleeping river
Thames. The vagrants shuffle into marked chosen
doorways with their newspaper blankets and
cardboard walls, which they zealously and jealously
guard, newspapers, cardboard and doorways, that is,
to settle down for the night, so much litter swept to
one side, so much misery wrapped in paper and tied
with string.

In Temple, haunt of barristers and clerks and
worried litigants, the gas lamps sing their litany of
warmth and light to nothing but empty courtyards
and silent Chambers. The drinking place alongside
the great City church lets its lamps invite in those

202

who have money to buy their way to oblivion, if that be their wish, but who close early most nights for lack of custom.

Into that strange half-haunted world come the non-people.

The City, graveyards, buried rivers and deep sewers once worked in by men called toshers who searched the murky disgusting depths for money, rags, bones and any other treasures that could be found, is a natural place for the non-people to live. Their homes have long since been disturbed, their memorials left leaning against walls or built into the walls themselves, a token nod to their memory. They come seeking revenge and retribution and remembrance.

It is surprising how few know that the body-snatchers plied their trade there, resurrecting corpses for the anatomists in the great City hospitals, especially Barts.

Few know that among those who called themselves non-people are those who live on blood. Non-people who take on the cloak of humans in order to get what they want and need. Humans that are mostly ignored or scorned.

Those who trespass into the City at night find this out at their cost – the ultimate cost, their lives.

The night was drawing in when Karl stumbled into the City from the West End, drunk, heartbroken and lost. He had one thing left in his pocket, the ring his bride-to-be had thrown in his face during a bitter argument in St James's Park. She had stormed off in one direction; he had stormed off in the other direction and sought consolation for his sorrows in the nearest pub. He then ended up walking without realising or even caring where he went. The words they had thrown at one another over some stupid, infinitesimally small item were of such bitterness and ferocity it was clear they could never speak to one another again. Somewhere in his drunken stupor, Karl realised that it was not the item which had caused the row but long built up tensions which had finally exploded. Better before the wedding than after, he tried to console himself.

It didn't work.

The City was quiet, only his heels disturbing the night as he stomped his way down Cheapside, heading for who knew where? Alone in a city of towering heartless buildings, shuttered and barred for the night, offices which held the secrets of millions of people in its archives and databases, vaults which held wealth beyond belief, especially those of the jewellers in Hatton Garden – ah, if he only had the skills to break in, to handle the beautiful gems and elegant pieces, if only, if only...

In a moment he was stone cold sober. The ring in his pocket seemed to be burning its way through the cloth, heating his skin. He pulled it out and went to throw it, but stopped. The diamond was worth something, the gold was worth something, why throw it away? Why not choose someone worthy of having it as a gift ... one of these vagrants, stinking and snoring in a doorway? Why not be truly magnanimous and give the gift of a lifetime to someone, change their future forever? Well, perhaps that was going a little too far but still...

He had no need of it. He could not bring himself to walk into a jewellers and sell it, for they would know what had happened and pride, that all enveloping sin, would not let him do that, not allow someone to smile sympathetically and wish him better luck next time. Best to give it away and start over again – if there was a next time.

But which one of the human flotsam could he give it to, why was one more deserving than another?

Random luck, he told himself, like winning the lottery, sometimes they draw the lucky number, the rest of the time, for some, the rest of their lives, they don't.

He stopped by a particularly savage looking drunk, long grey hair tied back with string, huge shaggy beard, incredibly lined face and gnarled twisted hands clutching the newspaper tightly to his body. The night was not cold, but habit dies hard.

'Hey you!' Karl nudged the sleeping man with his highly polished shoe, provoking a grunt that could have been 'clearorff' or something vulgar. He couldn't quite make out the words. He tried again. 'Look, I've got something for you.'

The eyes flicked open and for a moment Karl felt intense fear for they were black and soulless. Then the man blinked and the face changed.

'What'd'r'yer want then? I was kipping.'

'I want to give you something. I don't want it any more, it's worth a lot of money and I chose you to give it to.'

'What is it?'

'This.'

Karl held out the ring and the man took it, suspiciously turning it every way he could.

'What's the catch?'

205

'No catch. I broke up with my fiancé and that's it, end of relationship. I don't want to sell the ring; I want to give it to someone else to sell.'

'No one gives someone sommat for nuffink. What do you want me to do for it?'

'Nothing.' Karl was beginning to despair; the man was not grateful, just suspicious. 'Look, it's not stolen or anything, just take it and in the morning see if you can trade it for money to help you live.'

'Now who's gonna believe I got this legit?'

Karl was baffled. It was something he hadn't thought of, not for a moment. Of course, how could someone looking and smelling like that walk into a jeweller's and trade the ring for cash?

He made up his mind in that moment. 'All right. I'll remember you. I'll be back in the morning. I'll sell the ring myself and bring you the money.'

The teeth were stained and black but they still showed themselves in a grim smile. The vagrant grabbed Karl's arm in a tight vicious grip. 'I'll wait for you.'

'I will be back.'

'Don't you rat on me! You don't promise me a lifeline and then rat on me. I'll wait for you.'

Nodding, Karl stuffed the ring back in his pocket and walked swiftly away. He knew the doorway he knew the man, he would return.

He thought.

Taxis disappear at night from the City, for there are no passengers to hail them and be taken to distant destinations. The taxi drivers can make a killing by driving by theatres and nightclubs instead. Karl knew he would have to get the

206

Underground to go home. Mansion House, perhaps? But his footsteps were not taking him to an Underground station. He didn't quite know where he was going, it seemed drink and sorrow were combining to send him wandering aimlessly down narrow streets that held menace in every darkened window and doorway, taunted him with glimpses of civilisation, street lights and occasional cars, but he could not quite make his way to them.

He stumbled into what he thought was a small park, until he saw the gravestones around the walls. *Oh what the hell*, he thought, *I'll just...*

The morning sun touched his red rimmed eyes and woke him. Dishevelled and hung over, he somehow staggered to his feet, trying to brush dirt and early morning dew from his once fine suit. His throat was raw and his stomach screamed for something, anything, to stop the sick feeling which was consuming him. Too late, it had to come out.

'Sorry,' he muttered to whoever the headstone commemorated. 'You know how it is...'

He reached for a handkerchief and realised the pocket was empty. The ring had gone. Somewhere in the dark hours someone had robbed him, his wallet, his watch and the ring had gone.

'NO!' he roared into the silent morning, startling the birds into frantic squawking song in the trees. 'NO!' Fear gripped him, turning him to ice. He saw the soulless eyes of the vagrant, heard the menace in the voice, 'I will wait for you.' A voice that in that moment was not that of a vagrant drunk, but a cultured being, one with strength, one with purpose ... one who meant what he said.

I have to go and explain...

Was that not foolish? A sane voice in his head questioned the decision. The man knows not who you are. Go home. Walk if you must. Report the theft to the police at least, get them to take you home. Forget the vagrant.

'I will wait for you.'

He couldn't. Something was drawing him back to the doorway, to the man whose life he promised to change – and would dismally fail to do so.

Somehow he got himself moving; somehow he knew he had to find his way back. He had no idea where he was, but he thought if he let his subconscious work out the direction, he would be there in no time, not like the meandering aimless walk he had taken the night before. That was nothing but a jumbled memory anyway.

The sour taste of vomit in his mouth, hair awry and clothes wrecked, Karl staggered into the street and began to walk, letting his feet take him where they would.

And sure enough he was heading back to the building he remembered. And sure enough the vagrant was there, sitting up, alert, anticipating.

'Too damn early for you to have sold the ring,' he growled as Karl walked up to him. 'And you look like sommat the dog brought in from the dump.'

'I ... fell asleep in a graveyard last night and someone robbed me.'

'Right. Good story. Some ghoul came out of his grave and took the ring, did he?'

'Ring, wallet, watch, everything.'

The vagrant began to laugh. 'Right, mister, like I believe that story! Going back on your promise, then, are you?'

'I can't – I need to go home. I can find money and bring it back to you. I promise!'

The man stood up, towering over Karl. He had not appreciated how tall the man was; curled up in the doorway he looked small, almost insignificant. Now he revealed himself as over six foot and broad with it. The fear Karl had experienced in the graveyard was nothing to what he felt in that moment.

"You know what the old highwaymen used'ta say, dontcha? Your money or your life. You tell me you got no money, so-"

Karl's lifeless, bloodless body lay in the doorway for several hours before someone found him and reported the death to the police. The autopsy revealed not a drop of blood remained in his veins.

Victims of War

Thomas Hartwell

Do you not think a train whistle is the loneliest sound in the world?

Or is it just that I think so, because I am here on this station – because trains are my life?

Have you not seen them, the young men in khaki, hiding their fear behind gallows humour and stiff upper lip, when you know well they are not old enough to leave home, to face the guns, the foe in all their fierceness to push us out of Europe...

I see the men; I see the light around them. I can tell before they go who will come back missing a limb or even two, for those limbs have no light around them. I could go to them and say 'don't go, don't go, for you will come home legless, armless or wounded in some terrible way. But they would laugh at me and get on the train anyway.

But the real nightmare I live with day after day is the ones I see with no heads, just a skull Oh yes, I see the ones who will not return and how sad, how heartbreaking sad is it to see them for are they not young and energetic and have much to give to this world?

How many are so shown to me? I cannot say. In a crowd there could be 3 or 4 of them, maybe more. I see the skulls; I turn away for I cannot bear the thought of the loss of the young men.

The draining of the country is how I see it. Those who would work, those who would labour, those

210

who would teach, those who would lead, they are heading for the Front, that mystical ever moving ever dangerous and treacherous Front, where they will come face to face with the enemy, with gunfire, with barbed wire and with every fear there is known to man.

They will come home damaged in body and in mind.

So you see me, a porter here on this station, ushering the young men onto the trains, smart in their uniforms, casual in their humour, dying inside with fear and gut wrenching longing not to be there, someone they ignore completely. I wave my green flag, I blow my whistle; I send the train out of the station to the coast where they will board the ships that will take them into Hell and damnation. For they will return changed beyond belief, beyond recognition, except for those who wear the skulls, who will end up under grass in a foreign land.

Those who boarded those trains are the lucky ones. Those who stayed behind suffered the agonies of being left behind.

I wanted to go. I thought I had to go.

But I looked in the mirror the day I was due to go to the recruiting office, I looked and I saw –

A skull.

And I could not go.

I stay here, with my cowardice. In my own hell.

Back Where I Belong

Richard Laymon

It's dark in here. Too dark for me to see anything. I'm restricted in my movements, why can't I sit up, move my arms about, lift my head ... and what's this strange silky stuff I'm lying on? What's this hard pillow I am resting on...

I don't like this. Any of it. Not one single tiny miniscule scrap of it. Something's wrong and I want to know where and why and how and what and I want to know *now*. Not tomorrow, or next week, or next year, but NOW!

TALK TO ME!

Nothing. It's as if I'm in some kind of box...

I am, aren't I, in some kind of box. A coffin, to be precise.

What else is lined with silky stuff and holds my arms and legs and body in a rigid position where I can't move around and...

But I'm not dead!

Hold on, think this one through. Sensibly, logically, one step at a time.

I was...

Where?

In my car. Right. First step, in my car. Driving from/to?

Work. I remember. Driving from work, after a long day. Tired. Trying to keep my eyes open. Remember ... some idiot cutting in front of me and me too tired to react quickly and I smashed into him. I remember nothing else.

So, did someone declare me DOA? If so, I've been a long time waking up, there would have been an autopsy – hold on – can I feel – yes I can – and then a funeral and they don't happen very quickly and –

I guess I got buried, because I'm not burned up and ash and scattered somewhere or left in the bottom of the incinerator or stuffed into someone else's urn.

But you see, I'm NOT dead.

I need to get out of here. So, how do I get out of a) the coffin and b) the grave...

By sheer hard work.

Wow, that was hard work too!

Oh hell. I've been dead longer than I thought. The headstone's in place already. No, not already, look at the date, look at the date ... I've been dead a year. A whole long empty wasted do-nothing year.

But I look all right, what I can see of me, anyway. Not much rotting going on here, feet still got shoes on and nothing leaking out of the seams. The socks don't feel soggy either, so ... the feet must be intact. Right? The legs, let me look at the legs, tug up the trousers, well, would you look at that, pink flesh and blue veins and come to think of it, what about the hands which did the tugging? Well, would you look at that, too, all my fingers intact and heavens, she buried me with my wedding ring, too! I thought she would have had that off me and sold it immediately. Or do I do my cheating wife an injustice...?

213

Right. Head. Hmm, seems intact. Eyes, yes, nose, definitely, mouth with teeth, yes, and at least now I can say I will never have toothache again, hallelujah! Ears? Yes, I have ears. Hair? Longer than I normally have it but who's arguing about a small item like that?

Looks me as if I'm pretty well intact. Not bad for my age, as it happens. My age plus one year – obviously lying around underground does wonders for the body. Look, no paunch. That's the death starvation diet for you, works every time. I might market that, when I get myself back into civilisation.

And the bitch's house.

Now, let me orientate myself.

This is the large new burying ground, so my home is – several miles away. Well, I obviously can't drive there and equally can't hire a taxi either; there's no money in these pockets.

Hold on, you fool, you're not thinking straight.

Would you, after a year underground? Asleep?

No excuse. Come on, think! How did you get out of the coffin and the grave?

By thought.

Precisely.

Now think yourself at home.

Ha! Is it that easy, I ask myself... there is only one way to find out... isn't there?

And here I am walking up the path. She's made a few changes, that black-hearted wife of mine. The flower beds are all shrubs, no colour, no charm. Where's the central rose bush gone? Pride of my life, that was. What's a conifer doing in its place?

214

The door's a different colour. I preferred the green; don't like this – this wishy-washy blue. That's not a colour for a front door, that doesn't say 'look at me, I am proud to be the entrance to this home.' This one says 'I'm all delicate pastels and femininity and be kind to me.'

I will, when I get in.

Sudden thought, no one appears to have seen me yet. Was I lucky or am I invisible? I will find out when I-

Shocked look, smashed dishes, hand over mouth, eyes like saucers – I thought that was a stupid expression until I saw her eyes go as big as saucers when I walked into the (disgustingly yellow) kitchen.

'You...'

'Me.' I don't think I have a voice, leastways I didn't hear anything. Telepathy, perhaps, because her eyes got even bigger, if that was possible and it had to be, because they did.

Stop it with the foolish thoughts.

'It is you.' She's shaking head to foot, nerves, fright, love? Never the last one, never, never. I know my wife and a lot of memories are creeping back. Well, I've only been out of the grave for – how long? Half an hour? Taking me a little while to get myself together. Only natural.

Let's think about the reason I was so tired and couldn't react properly in the accident. Let's think about the flask she gave me to take to work, the drink which tasted just the tiny bit *wrong*, think about the look of sex she carried from time to time when she hadn't been with me. Think about the lies

215

... oh the lies ... I uncovered from time to time without her knowing.

Think about how she will react when I say the next words to her.

And smile.

'Darling, I got tired of lying in the grave. I decided to come back where I belong.'

Blood On The Rose

Kathryn Howard

You see me not.

How could you see me? I am no more than the morning mist which rises from the dewed grass as the sun touches it at dawn. I am no more than the fleeting touch of a spring breeze as it passes by your face and you reach out to touch it only to find it gone. I am no more than a name in history even if that name does resonate with you in your lessons on monarchs of the past. No one knows the truth but those who lived then, those who walked, talked, cried, laughed and loved. Oh, how we loved!

The sorrow of it is, the heartbreaking truth of it is, we loved the wrong people.

I loved the wrong person.

It is 469 years now since I laid my head on a block and had it severed from my body. 469 years I have had to regret my actions – but you will note, you who seek the fleeting breeze and the touch of mist at dawn – I said I have had the time to regret, not that I do.

It was my Uncle Norfolk's fault, he encouraged and coerced and in the end, blackmailed and blustered me into attracting His Majesty's attention. It was not difficult, a saucy glance, a bounce of curls, a hurrying away with breasts moving and thighs pressing the silks I wore, skirts lifted enough to show slender ankles, knowing his eyes were firm fixed on me and he was mine for the taking.

217

But I didn't want to take him.

Know this; then he was not a fine handsome king but an old man, to me anyway, carrying much weight and much illness. The sore on his leg smelled as if a doorway to hell had been left open after the bodies had been in the fire for a while; his smile was an array of teeth and no teeth where the apothecary had removed the bad ones and all in all, I have to say, what was left to be considered was the fact he was King Henry VIII, that I could be queen and have endless clothes, jewels and money.

Was it enough? I pondered this long into the night, tossing and turning in my bed until my curls were tangled and my bed a snarled mess of coverlets and pillows punched out of shape. In the end, family avarice overcame my scruples. It will not be long, they told me, he will die and you will be rich. And so will we.

You hear me not.

I speak but the words are no more than the rustling of the grass or the crunch of the gravel as you walk. I can speak and I do now speak of my love, my Thomas, my life, my soul, who I had to reject to marry His Majesty and how I could exchange one huge body and stinking ulcer for the slender strength, the cleanliness and the arms of Thomas Culpeper is beyond me even now, as I think on it.

Know this, though, I did my duty as wife and Queen. Did I not let him fondle my young body before others at banquets and the like, did I not control my face when he released the wind from his bad digestion and filled the room with a smell almost as bad as his ulcer, did I not let him lean on me when he could not walk well because the leg was paining him so? I did all this and so much more. Can you begin to understand how it felt to ride this gross body, to feel his thrusting, to know I could become pregnant by a man I had fast learned to hate with a deadly burning hatred?

And yet he was kindness itself. He thought of me, he treasured me; he called me his rose without thorns. I had clothes and jewellery finer than any I had ever possessed in my life. I had fine apartments and servants and my Lady Rochford as companion, I had horses and squires and all would bow down before me and grant my every wish. And that of my uncle, too, soon the family had the honours they so wished. And I cried myself to sleep every night in longing for my Thomas.

Why do you not sense me?

I am the presence that haunts the grounds of Hampton Court, where I could find happiness for a while, where I could walk with those I loved and feel the touch of their fingers folded around mine, see their smiles which were radiant and their faces which were full of love.

Warn me not of the Lady Rochford. How naive was I not to think she would seek revenge for the killing of the Boleyns, how swiftly did she introduce the thought I could bed with Thomas and not let His Majesty know a thing. So I did and I had nights of pleasure and days of anxiety, fearing not for myself but for those I loved so dearly. I am right glad, even now, that she followed me to the block, for did she not corrupt my life and my thoughts

219

entirely? Did she not lead me astray? And did I not go willingly, fool that I am?

Of course he found out. Of course the court is nothing but the biggest gossip place in England and soon enough my husband, the king, was presented with a record of my infidelities.

He sent that sour faced Cranmer to tell me I was confined to my chamber; he told me too that my beloved secretary Francis Dereham and my lover, Thomas Culpeper, were at the Tower. I knew all was lost for they would have been tortured – my love, my life, my Thomas, in the hands of the torturers! Was ever love such a painful thing?

They moved me from here to Syon Palace but a prison is a prison for all that.

They tore my lover's body apart, hanged him and held up his guts before his eyes and that day I knew true desolation. That day I knew I wanted to die, that there was no reason to live, that even if I could have persuaded my husband the King to let me live there would have been no life in me. So why even try?

Do you sense me now, oh visitor who comes to idle away the hours in a stately home beyond your imagining? For then we knew how to live, with magnificence and with wealth, did we not?

The time between my imprisonment and my execution was a thousand years – in my mind. They tell me now I went bravely to the block, but when love dies, when your only love dies, what is there left to live for?

Now tell me, visitor who knows me not at this moment, how do I find my Thomas? His body was cut into four and taken to the four corners of

London. His head was impaled on a pike. But where is Thomas himself? I can find him not, though I search Hampton Court endlessly, endlessly, looking for him.

I bid you, if you can at all see hear or sense me, be compassionate with this lonely queen who only sought love in the arms of the man she loved beyond all reason, help me find my one love.

I can, at times, create a single drop on the perfect roses in the gardens.

Tell him he will know where I am by the blood on the rose.

Will You Walk With Me A Way?

Edith Wharton

Will you walk with me a way?
Not far, just to the end of this road.

I am...empty inside and need a few moments of interaction with someone. Oh my, that sounds so formal, doesn't it? In truth, though, to ask you for a few moments of idle chatter, or gossip would be nonsensical. Especially with what I have in mind.

You look wet, is it raining? Oh I see; it's that fine drizzle that no umbrella can ward off, so you didn't bother. Me? No, I don't get wet. Call it a shield if you like, rain tends to avoid me.

Tell me, how are things at the nursing home these days? Does the garden bloom as fine in spring and summer as it used to? I recall the days of sitting out there, listening to the birds that would be singing as if their lives depended on it, the insects buzzing and flitting hither and thither as if their lives depended on it … come to think of it, they did. But us, the static ones, we stayed where we were, in our wheelchairs or sun loungers or wherever the staff had put us, there to bake in the heat until they took us back into the coolness of the home once more. Not a word of complaint from any of us, you know that, but oh the longing at times for shadow, cool water and rest from unremitting sunshine was overwhelming. But it was life and despite its many, many drawbacks, we clung to it tenaciously. Why? I wonder now why I did not just give up and drift away.

The big problem really, for all of us, is memories.

They hurt.

'Sometimes memories walk a little hard.' The wisest words I ever heard, from the most wonderful person I ever knew, my maternal grandmother. Oh she was right! How hard do the memories walk when your means of perambulation is either wheels or a walker? You recall the times when three strides would take you to the door, the cupboard, the TV, whatever/wherever. You recall the way you could walk freely down the road, wander round the shops, visit restaurants and museums, libraries and stately homes. Can you even begin to imagine not walking?

Of course not.

It doesn't come to all of us but enough … oh yes, enough.

But look at me now. Do I not walk well? Proud, tall and easy? Not so much as an ache in the hip joints or knees, the ankles flex and move as they should. Ah, the joy of it.

You? You are too young still, in terms of experience, to fully understand the joy I feel at being free to walk again.

I have to ask … do you not remember me? The old cantankerous lady who sat in her wheelchair in the garden and demanded cool drinks and ice cream and got neither? Do you not recall how I asked for shade and had none offered to me? Do you not know the suffering you put me through, you who were paid to care and didn't?

Well, I got you to walk with me a way. And look, here we are, right by the cemetery which is now my home. Oh, you will not escape me this time! Now I see the horror on your face as I cast off the mask of humanity and show you what I am. A skeleton.

Bony hands can grip harder than flesh covered ones, can't they?

Will you walk with me a way? Let me show you where I lie, here in the cold earth, with not so much as a snowdrop to lighten the darkness of the earth. No one cared, did they … and you, you were one of the worst. Did I not see you laughing behind closed doors at those who pleaded for respite from sun and thirst and were ignored?

Oh, you did not know, did you, that after I left your side of life I returned, over and over again, to watch, to record, to – all right, stalk you if you like.

Here we are. This is my narrow bed.

Will you share it with me for a while?

Like, eternity?

The Perfect Crime

Roald Dahl

I followed him home.

Intrigued, totally intrigued, I had to find out what it was he was doing – something was escaping me and I could see everything, usually.

I followed him home and wished that I had not done so.

Where were the steam trains? Where the huffing and puffing of the great engines, the smell of metal, coal and warm water drenching us who stood and waited for the moment we could reach for the heavy doors? Where the sound of the driving rods turning and turning and turning...

Fenchurch Street Station was not the same. It had become soulless, computerised; unfortunately not voiceless. The endless announcements, mostly unintelligible, had not changed. So much for technology, I thought.

He stepped through the space that I assumed would be a door at some point, looking for a seat. There were a few, next to large people or noisy people or those with strange wires in their ears and an equally strange bomp-bomp noise coming from somewhere. He sighed. It was that or stand and I had no idea how long this journey would be. I had no experience of these new trains, which looked like nothing I had ever envisaged before.

In the name of Heaven, had I been dead *that* long?

He and I worked together when we were fresh and vital and new and ambitious. Worked in the great City of London where fortunes are made and men can look for promotion, bonuses and a secure future, if you played your cards right and if you were the type of person whose face fitted.

Mine did not.

I was unaware of this at the time. I knew only that I worked hard and got nowhere and he worked hard and got everywhere. I knew too that he was using me, my skills, my ideas, my projections, knew that he was presenting them to the bosses in charge in fancy folders with elaborate headings, presenting them as if they were his own. Some were taken up, some were highly successful. He was promoted, I was not. He went to expensive lunches with bosses, I ate at the local corner place or sent out for takeaways to eat at my desk and persevere with the mundane work I had as my employment whilst my mind ranged far and wide and gathered what it could. I presented my proposal and had it dismissed. In a drunken moment after work, before we both staggered into Fenchurch Street Station for the train home, I told him of my idea.

Two days later the company applauded the new project and vowed to set it in motion within a week.

His face fitted, mine did not.

I was a fool back then. A complete fool. I saw his friendship as something I needed at all costs and ignored the stealing of my ideas. I accepted with humble gratitude the bonuses he gave me out of his much larger ones. It was only later I discovered he also got royalties – that was never mentioned. I accepted his gifts of money and his smiling handshake, his invitations to dinner, drinks and golf, as if they were sent by God Himself.

A new secretary arrived. She was supposed to be mine but he muscled in and before long I was back to writing my own reports, hammering them out on an ancient typewriter with a worn out ribbon. And lots of whiteout to go with it.

It wasn't that as much as the fact she was stunning. Natural blonde, huge eyes, huge – you get the picture. I wanted her. I dreamed of her. I lusted over her.

He got her.

I got an invitation to the wedding – declined it, pleading a prior engagement, sent a large gift from some department store or other – and spent the weekend in the country, walking, slamming a stick into the ground at every step and bashing the blossom from every hawthorn I saw.

It didn't help.

Friendship became hatred. Rivalry became open warfare.

Unspoken hatred and concealed open warfare, if you see what I mean. No one else commented so no one else knew.

He did and so did I. The innocent wife did not. 'That nice friend' she called me within my hearing when she thought I did not hear. I did, and I heard the snigger from him, too.

That was the moment his fate was sealed.

Planning a murder is not easy.

You have to ask yourself first where, then what with or quite simply how, then how you are going to walk away and not be discovered. Life behind bars is not a pleasant prospect.

I researched poisons. It seemed the obvious way, to me, anyway. It took some time but eventually I found what I was looking for and – at great cost – acquired some. Then I had to entice him to my place. That was difficult. I lived in a cheap bedsit, he had a 5 bedroomed out of town house. I had a clapped out old car, he had the latest model. The more I thought on the differences between us, the more I determined to dim his lights and end his life. It should have been me with the bonuses, the big car, the big house and the big wife – who by then was big with child.

His child.

In my mind it should have been my child. I who had no wife, no woman, no child. No life.

Ah but if I disposed of him, she would perhaps turn to 'that nice friend' and I could quietly assume his role in her life and that of the office.

Perhaps.

Why didn't I suspect anything? He came too willingly to my home, sat and chatted of work and life and his forthcoming son, he knew it would be a boy, he said, someone to take over when he was no longer here. He sipped the drink I poured him. He said he could stand another. It was the 'another' which I dropped poison into.

Did I mix the glasses, or – as I now believe – did he have demonic powers? Whatever, about an hour after he left, perfectly fit and healthy, I began to go into spasm, my heart pounding and threatening to leave my body via its bony cage, I had no chance to reach the telephone... I had no chance...

What demon woke me from my endless sleep? What evil influence told me that revenge was mine, after all these years, should I need it, want it, demand it even. I knew at that moment that I did and in that moment I was out of my grave and heading for the City of London before I had a chance to formulate any kind of plan.

Do you need a plan when you are a spirit, albeit one bent on retribution? No, you wait on chances.

I followed him home.

He was heavy, lumbering, grossly overweight, his face podgy but still painted with avarice. His wife, she who I lusted for, was heavy, lumbering, grossly overweight and vapid to the point of impossibility. Life, riches and good living had aged them both, changed them from the slender up-and-coming people I had so bitterly envied to these caricatures of richness. The house groaned under the weight of antiques that were bought for their value not for their beauty. I almost left him at that point, knowing that life had not given him the rewards he hoped for, unless of course he called this standard of living 'life'.

But no. My life for his? His life for mine?

I left him there, in his over-priced over furnished ugly home with his over-priced, over decorated now ugly wife and went back to my grave, my only home. There I sat on the long grass which no one had cut in an age, musing at the lack of inscription on my headstone, contemplating my old friend and enemy.

Murder will out. Someone said that a long time ago. He had to let the world know he had murdered me.

How and where and why ... the same questions I had the day I decided to murder him.

I was at the offices before he arrived, surprised yet not surprised to find he was second only to the head of the corporation. Not surprised to find lush beautiful offices and an equally lush beautiful secretary. I wondered if he was –

Then decided it mattered not if he was. I needed to secure his confession and end his life. That was all that mattered. Then I could return to my grave and sleep until Judgement Day was called, and hope that God would pardon me for following through an eye for an eye.

He arrived late. He knew I was there, no, he knew something was there for he kept looking round his office in surprise and – I was pleased to see – fear.

I wondered how much I could influence him. I tried making him pick up a pen. He did it. I tried getting him to write. He did it.

After that it was easy. With the sweat of fear running down his fat face and into the fat man sized collar he had on the fat man sized shirt, he wrote his confession, sealed it and put it in his desk.

I stood back, content that Part One had been achieved.

All I had to do was follow through with Part Two.

Then he surprised me.

In a hollow scared voice he asked if I was there and if I was, he asked for forgiveness. He said he had so much to live for – as if I hadn't! – and it was him or me.

Crawling, pathetic wimp. To think he could get round me like that!

I stayed there all day, sending cold chills at him, watching the sweat burst out on his forehead, watching the fear eating his entrails, the mistakes he made in his work, blaming it on the computer not on the fact I was looking over his shoulder and laughing at the mess he was making, even if I did not understand what he was doing or what the machine was capable of.

Oh the joy of sweet revenge! I let him sweat all day and walked with him to the station, through the City commuters, through the homeless and beggars who seem to haunt such places. We got to the platform and waited, with what seemed like hundreds of others, for the monstrosity that calls itself a train.

As it came into the station, I pushed him.

As he fell, he caught hold of me.

Together we ended up on the line and together we -

Santa's Special

Richard Laymon

"All aboard! All aboard!"

The steam engine clanked and groaned as if anxious for its bones, ageing as they were, then puffed steam into the bitter winter air, along with a cloud of very fine grit.

Doors slammed, children shrieked in excitement, parents grinned inanely, reliving their childhood vicariously through their offspring. Late arrivals scrambled for a carriage, the porter waving at them, "hurry! Hurry!"

A silver shriek from the whistle, a wave of the green flag, one last word to the driver and the wheels began to turn reluctantly, finding their grip on the silver rails, the engine gathering its energy and beginning its journey through the silent, frost covered countryside. The whistle screamed before the train entered a tunnel, clear warning to whatever was in the darkness to get out of the way. Picking up speed now, swaying from side to side on every curve and bend, the wheels spelling out their own message, soonbetheresoonbetheresoonbethere.

Santa special, a fun afternoon ride on the steam trains after a tour round the Christmas display and a visit to Santa's grotto. What could be better on a cold sunny pre Christmas afternoon?

Another scream from the whistle, another tunnel and the message of the wheels changed to beafraidbeafraidbeafraid...

The sunshine vanished in a heartbeat, thick ominous clouds pressed down on the countryside and rain began to fall, hammering on the roof and windows. It was freakish red rain, streaking the glass, finding its way through gaps in the ceilings, dropping on to the passengers, so they shrieked and screamed even as the whistle did, for the rain looked like blood, smelt like blood, stained like blood.

Someone leapt for the communication cord, yanking on it hard.

Even as they shrieked and screamed, the door opened and the guard stood there, holding a machete covered in blood.

"Who pulled the communication cord?" he demanded.

Waiting For a White Knight

Richard Laymon

She weeps, the blonde one manacled to the wall in the dungeon. She weeps in helpless misery, for her hands are in the manacles and she cannot reach to wipe away her tears. I see her there; I see the way she crouches against the stone, cold though it is, afraid of the darkness. Who would not be? The darkness is fearsome in its solidity, dense shadows which shift and stir and terrify the imagination. She has an imagination, this helpless weeping girl, which does her no good at all. Creatures, she thinks, monsters, she thinks and she would be right.

'Tis best she does not know she's right.

Castles come with memories. The stones hold the thoughts, prayers and tears of those who built them, those who lived in them, those who were held in them, those who died in them. Touch any castle wall and it will tell you some of its secrets, if you stand long enough to listen. Not all, oh no, for there are some secrets so dark, so deep, so dangerous that none shall speak of them, especially the witnessing walls.

It is this way in this castle, deep in the English countryside, overlooked by many but revered by those who know. Those who work here, those who live here, those who work at shielding it from the eyes, thoughts and memories of those who live nearby, the sorcerer who dwells in its depths, who casts spells and who –

But some things, again, we cannot speak of, should not speak of, for fear of disturbing that which should remain undisturbed. The dust of centuries lies on some things, dust which should not be removed.

Do I trouble you somewhat with these comments? If so, I do not apologise. You need to know the facts of this castle. You may visit it one day, you may enter the portals and find yourself entrapped in its spell and need to find the way out again – if you can.

Let me tell you what I do when the visitors come. It pleases me to tell you these things. Forgive me; I have few people to talk to these days.

I say: *Welcome. Come in and look around, absorb the atmosphere. It has been here many a long year, this place, as you will realise from the complete lack of amenities. But then, those of us who live here have no need of amenities of any kind, so it troubles us not.*

They sometimes seem puzzled when I say this and I do not explain. Mystery is always good. There is also the point that – well, speaking frankly here, they are not going to leave anyway, so why tell them everything? We do not need amenities as we are not alive.

I tell them: *it is said a black knight built this castle. Black in the sense that he walked on the wilder side of magic, or so legend has it. Some say the castle grew into existence overnight, others say it look a week. I doubt either is true, but – I know this, he dabbled in the black arts and 'dabbled' is not good. It is a bad word anyway, it means to take lightly - and he did. It was his downfall, again if legend be believed. He became trapped in the dungeon he created and the creatures ate him.* Sometimes I leave off that last bit. Sometimes I put it in. It depends on my mood, not on the visitors.

I tell them: *He left this place to his son, who was just one year old at the time. He grew to be a black knight, too, no doubt due to the influence of those left to guard and tutor him.*

I know not whether any of this be true, it is many generations into the past and there is a limit to how far back one person can look to find their family line. But it is a good story, is it not? Especially when it could be true. Who is to say such things did not really happen?

Then a bit of stage management, if you like. One of our people will act as a ghost and cast a long shadow across the room. Then I can do my 'concerned host' act. I say:

Oh, did the shadow bother you? I saw you start as it crossed the room. A true shade, that one, a revenant, a ghost if you prefer. I like to use the old terms, it sits better in my mouth. Revenant, isn't that a good word for something ethereal and yet real? He once lived here ... but no more. Now he is the resident revenant and here to give you a fright. Why not? You enter a haunted castle; do you not expect to find it haunted? But of course you do.

And it is.

Where was I? Oh yes, the black knight. Imbued with all the knowledge the resident sorcerer could teach him, all that his tutors could teach him about the ways of the world, all that his armourer could teach him about how to fight – and win. Much learned he was, much learned and skilled in all the arts.

I move them on. *I say: This is the Banqueting Hall. We had it laid out as it would have been in that time, splendid, is it not? Replica food, of course, we cannot afford the real thing any more, though it sorrows me to say it.*

Then I say: *Now look in here ... oh, sorry, that's the steps down to the cellars. Well, now you're almost there...*

And they are in the dungeon before they know it. Sometimes they are observant and comment and I say: *That over there? Bones of the guests I had some time ago. Bodies decompose fast down here, must be something to do with the air flow.*

It is inevitable there is someone in the dungeon at the time, which leaves me free to say: *Now look, that's upset my first visitor/guest!*

This day I had a blonde manacled to the wall. I said to her: *Dear one, worry not. Carry on with what you were doing. Oh I know what you were doing all right... You were wishing and waiting for a white knight to come and rescue you. Your new friends here will be wishing for the same thing ere long. Perhaps you can combine your thoughts and produce a miracle. Excuse the laughter; I know well it isn't going to happen... but there is always hope, isn't there? As long as you live, there will be hope.*

I have the perfect exit line... *Now I must leave you. I hear more visitors...*

237

The dark is full here. Now I can rest, the daylight is demanding on one such as I. The sorcerer sets the spell aside for a short while, the castle became visible and the ants are drawn to the sugar, every time. It never fails. It does mean I have to be polite to those who visit' pretend to give them the guided tour, be the charming host they expect to find when they come here. How else can I get them into the dungeon?

While the blonde one weeps and the dark ones sit in rigid terror at the thought of that which invades the dungeons at night, I sit here beside the hearth with mulled ale and good meats whilst those who serve me wait their turn at whatever is left in the dungeon.

Tomorrow, the sorcerer tells me, the white knight will come.

I have reserved a special set of manacles for him. They are spiked on the inside. Ah, he will enjoy those...

After I have taken him to death's door, that is.

Oh yes, just like the blonde, I am waiting for the white knight.

And so are those who haunt my cellars and dungeons. White meat for creatures of the night.

Just one small part of my existence.

Beware the next time the sorcerer lifts the spell on my castle. It could be your turn to reside in the dungeons.

My suggestion is that you pass by on the other side of the road.

My wish - and my hope - is that you come in.

Endurance

Sir Ernest Shackleton

"MEN WANTED: For hazardous journey. Small wages, bitter cold, long months of complete darkness, constant danger, safe return doubtful. Honour and recognition in case of success. Sir Ernest Shackleton."

And they came. I didn't think they would, I made it clear in the advertisement that there was not wealth attached to what would be an ordeal, but they surprised me.

They came and signed up and when the time came, we boarded '*Endurance*', the very last ship of its type. A three masted barque with a keel 85 inches thick, sides cross beamed wherever it could be, massively thick bow, constructed for polar work. We got her cheap for our expedition to cross Antarctica from sea to sea via the South Pole. We got her cheap but she was not a cheap built ship. Greenwood and whole oaks went into her construction. She was magnificent, even if there were complaints of her rolling in the wild seas before we got to our destination. Too rounded, they said, too rounded for the waves, but she was built for ice, not ordinary Arctic waters.

With great excitement and high expectations we sailed out of Plymouth in blazing summer sunshine, everyone on the dock waving and calling good luck. I felt we did not need it, we would be just fine; the plan was that we would sail down to South America, restock and then go on round the islands and head into the waters surrounding the greatest continent on earth.

Antarctica.

Land of ice and snow, of mountains and plains, of penguins and raging ice storms.

What could be simpler than that?

I knew well there was something else in Antarctica, something I had mentioned to no one but God in my prayers, asking him to keep us safe from its ravaging mouth and claws. The stupid thing was - I had no idea if it had a ravaging mouth and claws because I had never seen it - but I knew it was there.

I ask you, what else slashed claw marks down my tent when I made that infernally long walk, the one which gained me my knighthood? And do not think for a moment that was in my mind! I did the walk because I wanted to be there, to experience the continent for myself, to see the ice and the mountains and the ravines. I had no thought in my head that I would be rewarded. It was a wonderful gift from His Majesty and one I have never truly accepted as being something I should have. Not that I would have turned it down! It helped a lot when setting up a new expedition.

I digress. I was talking of that 'thing' which I felt lived there. That which stole and gnawed our supplies so that we were diverted and Admunsen got to the South Pole before us. Or am I making excuses now for our failure to get there first?

What coaxed Lawrence Oates from the tent and into the blizzard? I do not believe he was in his right mind when he left, on God's oath I do not.

What called to me on a level I did not know I had? A siren call, come, come, walk into the whiteness, come, come, the ice awaits...

I resisted the siren call. I stayed with my men, my team, those I was committed to working with. I had reserves of strength some of the others did not. I say that without disparaging them, we are not all alike.

But it seems to me, considering it from this distance of time, those of us who volunteered to explore Antarctica were not like other men. I would say the same of the researchers who work there now. There are many places on this planet which would stand exploration; the seas are just one of them. Great caves, strange creatures and beautiful plants remain unexplored and yet, and yet, we are not drawn to them. We are drawn to the coldness, the ice, the wastelands, for truly nothing will ever flourish there, apart from the penguins who have evolved to withstand the worst of the weather. We, being mere humans, have not.

The word 'endurance' covers many things. The endurance of suffering the closeness of working with and being with Scott is just one. I found I could not tolerate the man and that was a shame, for in the conditions we found ourselves, all the dogs dying through illness and we being weakened by the conditions we were struggling with, there should have been a greater camaraderie between us. The endurance of coping with the bitter cold, the ice laden winds, the sheer enormity of the landscape presented to us. The fight to reach the top of Mount Erebus was unbelievable, a true test of endurance, but having achieved it, the view was spectacular, I do confess. Endurance in starving so another could live. Endurance in giving away mittens so another could have comfort. That was later, when we were icebound and the expedition was lost. Endurance, sustaining the goodwill of those you work with through the most difficult circumstances, keeping spirits high and morale at an all time peak.

Endurance, part of the family motto and the name I gave to the great ship *'Polaris'* which was to take us to our greatest adventure yet, the crossing of the continent from sea to sea via the South Pole.

And back to that which haunted the continent.

What manner of being could haunt an entire vast continent? That was the question which consumed my thoughts, no matter whether I was working, lecturing, campaigning or just being at home with my loving wife. Was it as malevolent as I believed it to be?

I believe I put human characteristics on that which was unseen and not physical. The slashes in the canvas of the tent could have been the result of ice shards in the storms. The damaged supplies could have been the result of the extreme weather we suffered. It need not have been a ravaging beast with teeth and claws, in truth, logic told me it could not be, for there were never any footprints of anything that size and there was no evidence of a diminishing penguin population, the only mammal the monster, if it were one, could possibly eat. The killer whales which haunted the great Bay of Whales were not easy prey!

Nothing such could live on Antarctica, a place of extremes. There was no shelter, no food, little water, everything a being would need to exist.

I was of necessity forced back to considering a non-physical being, an entity, a malevolent spirit, one which guarded Antarctica and resented us being there. That made a good deal more sense to me; in as far as such a concept can make sense. It defied all logic, but then such a being would do just that. I was a logical man, my thinking direct and straight lined but I had to accept that there were things I did not understand.

But I wanted to understand, so I went back to try and find 'it', to persuade 'it' to reveal something of itself to me.

It and the continent had other ideas.

We sailed into pack ice. I was used to ice but I had never seen any like this, so thick, so immovable. We were trapped almost immediately and my senses were alerted to the being which was obviously determined to stop us invading its land yet again.

Its voice was contained in the howling gales, its presence felt in the awful silences between the gales. I began to realise that the others sensed something too, at times they would stand looking out at the ice, at the continent we could just see but not reach, as if they were staring at something rather than nothing, for their gaze was concentrated, their eyes narrowed. Then they would shudder as if something had walked over their grave. Not a word was said, I think we were all too embarrassed to admit to even thinking of such a thing.

243

We held on somehow, in the face of great difficulties, hoping that when Spring came the ice would release the *'Endurance'* but It had other ideas. When Spring came, the pressure on the ship increased, despite its reinforced hull it sprang a leak and water poured in. We evacuated the ship and stood helpless as it sank.

Did I not hear gales of unnatural, inhuman laughter as she went down?

Or was that my sorrow at losing a wonderful ship – and my hopes with it?

How puny we were, alone on the ice, no ship, limited supplies, how much did I believe then that we were truly being forced to retreat, that whatever the being was, it did not want us there.

At times I longed to speak with the others of that which haunted my innermost thoughts at all times, but in such extremities as we found ourselves, I could not bring myself to speak of it. What would they think of me if I spoke of such a being? That their leader had begun to lose his mind in the whiteness and the vastness of the continent?

What then of my ability to lead? No, I kept the thoughts to myself and only now, all these years later, do I speak of them for the first time. With difficulty too, I freely confess. This story has been a long time in the telling, for it is not easy to rationalise that which cannot be rationalised.

I rescued everyone eventually, through a long process of going here and there and tramping for miles, all the time knowing that the being was laughing at us for being puny individuals. And perhaps we were – perhaps we are. There are research stations on the continent but no settlements, a few births to claim an area but nothing serious, in my view anyway. Antarctica remains what it is, an enigma, a place apart, dry, bitterly cold, unforgiving, mysterious.

In trying to return, I lost my hold on life. Now I visit Antarctica at will, always searching for that which drove me away.

One day I will find it.

The Hunger of the Moon

Virgil Grissom

Space is truly the final frontier. Dangerous, demanding, daunting, the sheer vastness of it is beyond the rational mind of any human being. Those who try to tell us how the Universe began haven't been out there and experienced the display of stars and planets unfiltered by our polluted atmosphere, haven't seen the glittering colours which defy description and categorisation, haven't begun to comprehend the sheer majesty and magnificence of our Universe (disregarding all the others that scientists believe are out there, beyond this one). If they had, they'd understand that the Universe is so mysterious that no person can ever discover all its secrets, let alone determine how it began.

I am saying scientists have their place in life, but they should keep to their place, not pontificate on that which they do not understand: the birth of the Universe.

I can say this with safety, for I'm not on your side of life any more. I can also say this with sure knowledge for I am one of the chosen few who have been in space more than once, someone who has been able to relive the glory of the panorama of the constellations. It's almost enough to make you forget what you're there to do; somehow tasks become insignificant when dwarfed by that incredible hugeness.

246

Imagine being sandwiched between the awesome moon and the even more awesome earth, catching sight of the whole panorama of space... it's enough to turn any man's head.

Those craters are *huge* and you could easily believe once they were full of water, plant life and creatures. Well, possibly I had an over-active imagination even then. It's gotten worse since I came into spirit life...

What impressed me most was the sheer desolation of that totally dead ball of rock. A true wasteland. No movement, nothing but scars and craters left by passing asteroids and space debris, nothing but bitter coldness and emptiness. It left a chill on my heart even in the short time I was able to observe it. This is why it has deeply affected those who walked on its surface. I envy them even now, those whose space suited feet scuffed that dust and stood on that rock, those who were able to look at earth from its nearest neighbour, those who fulfilled President Kennedy's challenge, for a man to stand on the moon. An American man to stand on the moon, forgive me!

The moon ... that which holds our imagination and seemingly always has done. From earth it appears almost benevolent, the craters forming a face when it's full, changing its contours as the earth turns. It's easy to forget that it's cratered, battered, a frozen wasteland of rock, endlessly circling the earth and doing no more than radiating to us the rays of the sun. It has no reason to exist other than that.

I asked myself often if it needs to have any reason for existence apart from that: my answer is no.

We could speculate for hours on whether the oceans would be better without being pulled back and forth; whether that would affect the way we live. Would it? What we do know is: we arrange our lives by the moon, our monthly calendar cycle is based on its phases, it gives light at night, it features in a million songs and poems; the great stone circles and avenues, what did they chart but the phases of the moon? I believe so, anyway. It's responsible for werewolves and other aberrations... I joke, possibly. We would surely be very unhappy without a moon.

My life ended very abruptly aboard a space vehicle that didn't leave the ground. For me there is immense sadness in that, I would have been more content to have died in space, out there where the stars are truly like diamonds, flashing colours you've never seen on earth. Out there where the curve of the earth itself is so fascinating you forget you have controls to deal with. Out there where the moon ... but that's where I plan to stop being factual and begin being fictional, the reason I came to talk to you. I've had a story in my head for a while and wanted to tell it. Now I have the chance...

The moon surface looked more pockmarked and battered than ever to the captain staring through the window at the landing point. No matter how many journeys he made, it was always a strange experience actually arriving on the barren ball of rock. The moon dome was happening, truly happening after many years of experiment and

248

argument, the conveying of supplies, both for the building and those working on the dome, was proving a long drawn out job. Only so much could be carried on each journey.

He felt a faint shudder as he landed the craft. It couldn't have been mechanical, at least he hoped it wasn't, the last thing he wanted was to be marooned on the moon until another ship arrived to take him and his crew back to earth. It was more like a moonquake, if such a thing existed. Others had mentioned the shuddering but dismissed it as no more than their imagination.

An odd thought came into his mind: the moon *was* dead, wasn't it?

He laughed off the thought. Of course it was.

Well, nothing had been discovered, anyway, and men had walked all over the ball of rock, dark side and light side alike.

The crew were suited up and out of the ship, at the cargo hatch and beginning to undo the bolts which held it in place.

The shudder became a lot stronger, more like an earthquake. Every helmeted head turned as one, as the ground opened up in what looked remarkably like a huge open mouth, one that was laughing.

As the ship, the men and the part of the dome began to slide into the crevice, the captain mused, in his last seconds of life, that there was a man on the moon after all.

And so my piece of trivial fiction is told. You like horror, it seems, and there is nothing so horrific – on the surface – as that which seems benign turning evil at the last moment. But there is something which is inherently more horrific than that, being enclosed in a capsule which is on fire and you cannot escape.

I say no more, but leave my death to your imagination. I know you have one.

The Day Death Wore Boots

Yul Brynner

The thing is ... I'm old enough to know better, old enough to know it isn't a good idea to stand looking in the window of an 'antique' shop and be taken in by a toy.

It's not like I'm lonely, is it? I mean ... I got a life, ain't I? Course I have. Go to work, talk to people, shop, talk to people, come home, cook my TV dinner which I eat in front of the computer – all right, I'm lonely.

But that's beside the point, really it is. I wanted the toy cos I wanted the toy, not because I don't have a life.

I've always loved Westerns, you see, the whole shoot-'em-up gunfights and ranches and outlaws and everything. And there's this toy, a whole town of it, a Western town with gunfighters and horses and ladies wearing flouncy dresses who are no better than they should be and there's the cattle outside the town and the cowboys bringing them in and there's the sheriff and the undertaker standing by because of the gunfight in the street and the men leaning on the bar outside the saloon and the whole thing was taking up the entire window display and I wanted it.

It would be silly money, of course, but I had silly money, not having much else to spend it on these days. No wife, no lover, no – nearly said it, didn't I? Nearly said 'no friends.' Well, it would be true.

251

So I went in and saw the old man selling the thing and said I wanted it. And he said no. It wasn't for sale. And I said, "oh yes it is; it's right there in the window and no sign to say DISPLAY ONLY and I want it."

And he says; this old guy with a peaked cap and twisted smile and when he turned, a big hump on his back like you would not believe, a true hunchback, poor guy and I wondered if it pained him at times, a twisted spine like that, he says:

"It's dangerous. I sell it and it comes back later with an addition. One I don't always like."

"Addition? Explain yourself, sir."

"Well, the sheriff wasn't there when I got it first off; he was there when it came back in. The gunfight wasn't there, now I'm worried that there's going to be a death, or something."

I laughed. I laughed until my stomach hurt.

"It's like model trains," I gasped eventually, when the convulsions stopped. "You add things as you go along."

"Maybe," he said, obviously unconvinced. "Maybe, but there's this – light that comes over the thing and it changes."

"I still want it," I said, determined to have it at all costs. A childhood dream, my own Western town to play with! Adult I might be, child I was inside. As we all are.

He shrugged. "I have to put up the arguments," he said. "If the customer persists, then I let them buy it. It's £2,500."

"Done."

He looked at me in shock. "You're not going to haggle?"

"No. I said I wanted it and I meant it."

"All right. Don't know how much I'll be able to give you when you return it, though."

"Return it? It's mine to keep forever!"

"I don't think so. No one's kept it yet and they all said that."

"I'm different."

"They said that, too."

The mood in the shop changed subtly; darkness crept in, a hint of – menace. I shivered and pulled out my platinum credit card. Best get this purchase done and dusted, I thought, and be out of there, taking my dreams of future evenings of happiness away with me.

The old man took the card as if it would explode in a moment of madness. "You sure about this?"

"I'm sure."

"Be it on your head, then."

The card transaction was soon done. How quickly and easily we can spend money with plastic! In olden days I would have counted out the money and he would have counted it again or I would have produced a gold nibbed fountain pen and written a cheque in an elegant italic hand. Instead I punched four numbers into a machine and it churned out a soulless slip of paper in return.

I wrote my address on the pad he offered me and arranged a delivery time for the following Saturday. I left the shop with his strange words in my ears and my mind.

"You'll be all right if you don't see the ghost light, Mister."

I almost turned back, almost wanted to grab him by the lapels and say 'if you don't want to sell the bloody thing, don't display it! Don't try and frighten people with silly notions! Take the money and be glad of the sale! Don't you know there's a recession in place?'

I didn't. I walked away, quickly. I walked away because I thought if I asked questions about the ghost light there might be answers I didn't want to hear. Or I would do some damage and the sale would be cancelled.

I wanted the Western town to play with.

I admit it. I had not grown up. Not by a long, long way.

***

Saturday was a long time coming.

It was Wednesday when the purchase was made. I had all of Wednesday evening, all of Thursday's endless 24 hours and all of Friday's 24 hours to live through and then, heaven help me, most of Saturday to get through, too. Impatient to have my Western town? Of course not. In denial, I know that.

But eventually the removal van was there. Four big overweight red faced men got out and began manhandling my precious town off the pallet it was on and working out how to get it over and around my garden gate, my front door, my stairs...but they did it with great ease and I wondered how many people had owned this precious toy before me and how many times it had been returned... I didn't want to ask. I didn't need to know. It was mine and that was all there was to it.

I had cleared the second bedroom for the town, arranged tables so that it would be at the right height for me to observe it. Do please note I did not say 'play with it', not then. I said it earlier but not when it arrived. Then it was serious. A hobby. An interest. Not a game.

They placed it on the tables. They gave me a box which they said held the people, horses and cattle. They bid me a happy time with my new acquisition and they left, declining any invitation to drink tea or coffee or alcohol. It was as if they could not wait to be free of the thing.

I shut the front door behind them and raced back upstairs, eager to place the people and animals in my new town.

They were already there. The box was on its side, the cattle were outside the town, the horses were tied up in front of the saloon, the men were leaning on the rail - ready to watch the gunfight which was about to take place.

I decided I was seeing things. I decided none of it was real; I had all evening to put everyone where I wanted them.

It was clear that the toys/dolls/whatever they were had other ideas.

Even as I stood there, open mouthed, the two confronting each other in the middle of the main street pulled their guns and fired. One fell down in a puff of smoke and dust.

I left the room.

I left the room to go find a bottle of whiskey and have several stiff drinks.

I did not see what I just saw. I did not see the dolls/toys/whatever they were actually do something by themselves.

I decided that I had to make statements which I would believe.

So I believed that they had not put themselves into the town.

They had not walked, talked and done something in front of me without my help.

Had they?

I went back upstairs, curiosity getting the better of me. Surely they were playacting, surely one had not been –killed – had it?

It was as if I wasn't there. None of this 'freezing when a human walks into the room' as we are led to believe 'real' toys did.

It was as if ... this town was real life. As I walked in the room I saw someone bending over the man on the ground, shaking his head. The undertaker wandered over and pulled out a tape measure. I couldn't believe it. He really was dead. He had to be. He hadn't moved, even when pushed around a bit. The man who had killed him had walked off. He was nowhere to be seen.

They talked. I know they talked, I saw their mouths move. I couldn't hear a word but I knew everything they were saying.

"He's a gonner, ain't he, Doc?"

"That he is."

"Do we know who he is?"

"Nope. Best get him buried in Boot Hill and hope no one comes asking. Big Dan's done it again."

I left the room for the second time. I had to be going out of my mind. There was no other explanation.

It took a good deal of courage for me to walk into the room again. Curiosity drove me there and the need to see the toy on which I had spent over £2000 helped me overcome my fears – to some degree.

I opened the door and edged in carefully. The men were gone from the saloon, the horses had gone too. The cattle had disappeared. No one was lying in the road. All was calm. It looked like a toy once again.

Except for the strange misty white light surrounding the whole thing.

Except for the blood stain on the sand in the middle of the road.

Even as I thought about it, a man came out of the saloon, walked across to the spot and kicked sand over it. He walked back into the saloon, the door swinging open just enough for me to see all the men at the bar and the tables, some gambling, some laughing, all drinking. The floozy behind the bar waved to me. I swear she did.

I remembered what the hunchback said about the 'additions' to the town each time it came back. There would be 'additions,' he said.

The truth was, this town was real, tiny but real and people would come and go. Even realising that, I could not come to terms with the fact I had seen a real gunfight and a real death.

A cart came creaking along the road, a rough pinewood coffin on the back. Two men walked alongside, carrying spades. They were going to bury the dead man.

Money or not, I went nowhere near the town for the whole of Sunday. I sat in my lounge with whiskey and loud music but it didn't muffle the sound of horses, wheels, cattle, men shouting, the occasional gunshot, shrieking giggling women and the ominous sound of spades hitting earth. I told myself it was all in my head. I told myself it was my wild imagination, everything I had ever read, watched, thought of, was happening right there above my head. In my mind.

It was in my mind, wasn't it?

Monday morning curiosity got the better of me. I went slowly up the stairs, afraid of walking around my own home. That was ridiculous. It was outrageous. I had spent good money on a toy and I wanted to play with it.

Said it for the first time, didn't I? Play with it. The hunchback hadn't told me I would be an observer to real life happenings. He treated it as an expensive toy.

Perhaps he didn't know.

What was the 'ghost-light' he was on about? I had to find out.

The town was quiet. There was one horse outside the General Store. It stood still, well, sort of, it was busy dropping turds into the road actually and I wondered, even as I watched, why no turds were seen in Western films. Did they hire someone specifically to clear them up the moment a horse dropped them? What sort of job was that? What sort of money would they get?

Someone came out of the General Store carrying a weighty saddlebag, the way it pulled him down one side it had to be heavy. He mounted the horse and rode out of town. Gone. Over the edge of the board the town was on and gone. Into – what?

There was mystery on mystery here.

I did what I should have done in the first place, got me a comfortable chair and sat down to watch the show.

The Sheriff's office door opened and he sauntered out, cigarette in the corner of his mouth, Stetson at a jaunty angle. He stood on the sidewalk/boardwalk/ whatever and surveyed the empty road. It was as if he was waiting for someone/ something, rather than keeping a watchful eye on the inhabitants of –

The town had no name. I had just realised that, with a shock. I could call it Dodge City but that would be too silly for words. I needed my own name.

"Smoke Town," I said aloud.

The sheriff turned round on his boot heels and glared at me.

"In the name of God, Mister, what sorta dang-fool name is that?" he shouted.

"Sorry." I waved a pathetic hand in his direction. "What's the town called, then?"

"Ghostlight."

I felt a shudder run the length of my spine. You can't call a town Ghost Light, surely?

"It's Ghostlight, Mister, all one word." The sheriff looked at me as if disbelieving I could be that stupid. Well, I guess I was; I bought the thing, after all. "And..." he added, taking off the Stetson and scratching his head, "you ain't dressed proper, either. Where's your chaps and Stetson and six shooter, then?"

"I..."

I left the room. I left not because I was disconcerted by an idiotic conversation with a sheriff who was a doll, an extra in a toy Western town, but because I had an overwhelming desire to 'dress proper'. I headed for my town, where people were a normal size and spoke in normal voices and took money for goods and they took my money for a complete Western fancy dress outfit, including gun and boots. The gun, they assured me, was a replica, which they were not supposed to sell under new gun laws but which they slid into the package because no true-blue-up-and-coming cowboy would be seen out without one.

I agreed.

I hurried home through the blazing sunshine, through the shoppers indifferent to my excitement and my anticipation and my fears, rushed into my house and went to change.

Properly fitted out, looking every inch the rough roustabout cowboy, I went back into the room to look at Ghostlight. My western town. My purchase. My possession.

If I said it often enough I would believe it – eventually.

The sheriff was sitting in a beat up old chair, balancing on the back legs which looked like they'd give way any minute. He looked up when I walked in and grinned.

"Better. Now Big Dan can come into town and meet you proper. He wouldn't want to see no dandy, would he?"

I sat down in my chair. "How much of this place does Big Dan own?"

"Most on it." The sheriff sucked on a cigarillo for a bit and then turned back to me. "How come no one else asked these questions, Mister? I mean, we been in some homes, for sure we have, but no one asked questions."

"What did they do, then? Just watch?"

"Nah. Run screaming from the room more times than not. You ain't done that. You're different."

I laughed. I could well understand people running screaming from the room. I had not exactly run but left rather sharp-ish a few times. "I'm intrigued," I told him. "How do you live and do things without what I can see as physical conditions?"

"Like?"

"Well, water and food and..."

"You got it wrong, Mister. Truth is; this is a town in a state in a country. You got just one bit of it, like a window, if you like."

"So, the gunfight was real, then?"

"Course it was. Damn outlaw coming into town looking for trouble, got shot down and got buried."

"Shot down by..."

"Big Dan."

"Does he own this town?"

"Sure enough does." The sheriff got up and stretched. "I'm through chattering, Mister. You got enough to think on for a while. I'm about to go get me a drink or two. I see old Ned heading this way on his ass; he's always good for a story or two. You ain't got no stories, Mister, just a load of questions. You'd be better done watching and not asking."

He ambled across the sandy road just as Old Ned, whoever he was, came into view on the far edge of the town – as far as I was concerned, anyway. Judging by the state of him, he'd travelled a good deal further than that.

I watched the old man shamble into the saloon, saw the sheriff greet him and as the doors swung back with a clatter – they were badly fitting doors, someone should sort that out for them – I saw the drinks being poured.

And I waited.

The singing started, then the fights, usual problems I expect in a Western town. Bodies spilled from the saloon into the street, spitting, fighting, falling down drunk but no one pulled a gun.

At that point, anyway.

That sort of came later.

You must forgive me; I am not entirely sure what happened then. I know I was tired and hungry and needed a bathroom visit and was reluctant to leave the town in case I missed anything.

Then I saw this guy, drunk as a skunk, for want of a better polite expression, staring at me.

"What you think you're looking at?" he snarled.

"Well, the town..." I answered, a bit sheepishly. Seemed a silly answer but it was the truth.

"Get yourself gone!" he snapped.

"I can't do that," I protested. "I bought this town and I'm entitled to look at it if I want!"

"Really?" He showed yellowing teeth in what passed for a grin. It didn't work. "The man with the gun says who's entitled!" and damned if a bullet didn't whistle past my ear and bury itself in the ceiling.

In a moment I pulled my gun and fired back.

And he fell down dead.

I stared at him. Stared at the 'replica' gun and wondered what the hell had just gone down there. And why.

The sheriff came out and looked at the dead man, then at me.

"Oh my," he said, so soft I hardly heard him."That's Big Dan's brother, Mister. You're in trouble now."

"It was ... they said ... supposed not to be a real gun ..."

It all sounded false even as I said it.

I knew he wouldn't believe me. Hell, *I* did didn't believe me, either.

I turned out the light and left the room before the misty ghostlight came and bothered me.

So you see, friend, if you've got all that down in your notebook, that's how it happened. Honest to God that's how it happened.

I got up next morning and found bars on my bedroom window and a lock on the door.

And the padre came to see me. Why was I not in the least surprised to see it was the hunchback from the toyshop?

He gave me a lopsided sort of smile. "It's coming back to me again, then," he said, looking round the room, swinging the bunch of keys from one finger. "With another addition."

"What's that?" I asked, stupidly. I should have known the answer.

"A gallows," he said. "They're hanging you in the morning."

Yul Brynner donned his Westworld outfit and came to stalk my office where he dictated this totally insane story with that evil grin he wore throughout that film. The rest of the time he's one nice person...

For The Greater Good

Dorothy Davies

"Shut the damn door, Crouch!"

"What's up, Joseph? Too cold for you? Get too hot in here and the stiffs'll start to rot. That what you want?"

"No, just some heat for them as are drinking, is all."

Ben Crouch studied the belligerent face of the landlord, wondering what the problem was this night. He'd had his share of the advance paid out by the surgeons to get the bodysnatching season underway, what else did he want?

'   "All right, look, the door's shut. Now if any of the medical students wants to come in and take a look at the stiffs, they better be quick about it 'cos if they start smelling we got problems."

Joseph Durham swabbed at the bar with a dirty cloth, a token gesture of cleanliness which fooled no one, least of all Ben Crouch and his cronies. Ale was poured into a thick tankard and pushed along the bar until the ex-prize fighter was able to grasp it and lift it to his lips. He spluttered and coughed. "In the name of all that's holy, Joseph, what the hell's that?"

"My best ale!" Joseph retorted. "Shows you got no taste, Ben Crouch!" A ripple of laughter went around the 'Fortune of War' pub. The regulars knew of the ongoing half-friendly, half-nasty banter between the two men; it had been going on for a long time. It seemed to get worse when the bodies were laid out in the back room, awaiting Sir John Abernethy's minions coming to assess the haul. Digging up bodies was not illegal, stealing a grave shroud was. Technically, the 'Fortune of War' was not acting illegally in displaying the bodies, but Joseph Durham was happier when they were not there.

Even as he thought this, the door opened and two medical students came in. One was new, his nerves showing even as he tried to hide them.

"Sir John asks..."

"Three big ones and one half size out back." Ben Crouch gestured with a sweep of the arm clad in a most elaborate jacket. The ruffles on his shirt showed, the lights in the public house glinted on his gold jewellery. He was the most dandified person in the place and stood out because of it.

The more experienced student made straight for the back room, the other hesitated in front of Ben Crouch. "You the famous prize fighter, Sir?" he asked with obvious awe.

"That I am, sonny! You heard of me then?"

"I have indeed, sir. My father has seen many of your fights and said you were one of the best. I am honoured to meet you, sir."

Ben Crouch seemed to grow several inches in all directions in the light of the compliment. A huge grin split his face and he grasped the young man's hand. "Right pleased I am to meet you, young man. Gonna be a surgeon, are you?"

"I would like to be, sir. I need to see how I get on with the dissection."

"Nothing to it," one of Ben Crouch's 'helpers' butted in. "A body's a body for all anyone ever wants to say to you about it. When they're dead they're just meat."

Ben Crouch realised the young man was beginning to go rather green, so he clapped him on the shoulder, turned him toward the bar and shouted, "give this boy a shot of the best hard stuff, would you? Put it on my bill."

A very small glass containing an extremely dark liquor was put on the bar and the young men took it hesitantly, looking at Ben Crouch for encouragement.

"Drink it down in one go," he advised, "then go take a look at the stiffs, go report back to Sir John and tell him we have a right good collection here for him this night."

The drink disappeared, the young man coughed and went very red in the face, but it seemed to give him courage. His associate was beckoning to him from the back room; he walked boldly over and looked in. "Look all right to me," he said, his voice slurring very slightly.

"But you haven't looked properly!" protested the student.

"Don't need to. Mr Crouch here says to tell Sir John he has a right good collection for him this night. Don't need to know any more than that."

It was obvious that the other young man was nerveless when it came to dead bodies. He looked at his slightly drunk companion with disgust. "We'd better get back then, seeing as how we have a message for Sir John himself."

The two young men left the pub. The drinkers waited until they were out of earshot before they broke into riotous laughter. Ben Crouch laughed so hard he had tears pouring down his face. "I never saw anyone drink your liquor like that before, Joseph! Good job he don't know what it is!"

Joseph Durham joined in the laughter. 'Tis naught but the dregs of all that gets left,' he said through his mirth. "And there was him thinking he had my best hard stuff!"

The door opened and everyone turned to look, expecting to see medical students come to take the bodies away. Instead the imposing figure of Sir John Abernethy stood in the middle of the room.

"Was that your idea of a joke, Crouch?" he demanded. "If it was, it was damn fool, that student is trying to project his stomach out through his mouth outside Bart's at this moment. He will soon find it a medical impossibility."

Joseph Durham wiped his eyes with the corner of his apron. 'Was but a small jest, sire, the lad were that green at the mere thought of the stiffs, we felt we had to boost his courage a bit."

Sir John's stern face cracked into a small smile. "I can see why you did it, but you must have given him some strong stuff for him to be vomiting it so quickly."

"While you're here, sire, take a look yourself at what we have the night." Ben Crouch moved quickly to cover up the moment, knowing they had played a mean trick on the student.

"I will, Crouch; that's a good idea." Sir John strode over to the back room and looked in. 'You were right, fine ones tonight, I'll get someone across

268

to collect them. We can get on with the dissection in the morning."

The surgeon walked out of the pub, leaving behind a sense of anti-climax. It had been a small joke, it was a shame it had such a violent effect so quickly, but on the other hand, Sir John had not made trouble over it, he must have realised himself that the boy was nervous, not having seen a dead body before. He must also have known that to send somebody so naive into the den of body snatchers was asking for trouble. Or so Ben Crouch reasoned to himself, as he could find no other explanation for Sir John's attitude. He sighed, patted the pocket where the guineas rested and thought bodysnatching was a good deal easier way to make money then prize-fighting had ever been. This way he didn't have to get hurt, he didn't have to train, he didn't have to pummel another man into the ground, just to use his cohorts to get them out of the ground and into Bart's Hospital, there to be dissected for the greater good of the rest of the population.

Feeling very benevolent at that moment, he threw a golden guinea at Joseph Durham. "Drinks for everyone," he said, just as the students arrived and took the bodies away.

Factual note: In one year 8 bodies went into Guy's Hospital in London for dissection and 137 bodies went into St Bartholomew's Hospital in the City of London. No contemporary books make reference to Sir John Abernethy's use of the body snatchers but it is a matter of record that Ben Crouch and his gang supplied the hospital with all that they needed in the way of 'raw material' for their anatomy lessons. Ben Crouch was known as the 'Corpse King'. Records show that Joseph Durham was indeed the landlord of the 'Fortune of War' public house at that time. The building no longer exists; in its place is a banking establishment which has a plaque set in one wall commemorating the 'Fortune of War' and its place in the bodysnatching story. When I researched the background for my novel on the bodysnatchers (still being written) my mother told me that her father used to drink in the 'Fortune of War' pub...

Now I Can See You

Richard Laymon

I wondered what sort of sight I was as I stood on his doorstep, waiting for him to open the door. Pretty horrific, I should think, with empty eye sockets weeping blood which trickled down my face and onto my clothes. I had one arm wrapped in duct tape around the arm of the chair which I had broken off in my escape efforts. He would not be pleased to see me, but he had something I wanted.

I heard the door open and the gasp of horror. I pushed at his unresisting chest and he backed into the hall. I sensed where we were going, pushed a bit more and he fell into the dining room, scrabbled to his feet and found a chair. Saved me the job.

I had duct tape in my pocket and, taking advantage of his shock, managed to tape him to his chair, only I did a better job of it than he had on me.

"Now," I said, through teeth that were bound to be bloodstained – it had been hard biting through the tape – "let's see how you like it!"

"I..."

"You what? Thought I would die, Mr. Optic, like the others? No such luck. You picked the wrong person this time. Where are my eyes?"

"Eyes ..."

"Those things you scooped from my head with my own spoon, remember? I want them back."

"They're..."

"They're what? Eaten? Played with? Thrown to the cat? What?"

271

"In a jar of formaldehyde."

"Oh. Right. Useless then."

I could smell his fear, along with everything else. I must have been more horrific in appearance than I realised. He had let go of everything. And I do mean everything.

"Then you owe me some eyes, Mr. Optic."

"Don't call me that!"

"Why? That's what the papers call you, isn't it? You collect eyes, right?"

"Well..."

"You probably have some boring suburban name which matters not right now. I want some eyes. I'll settle for yours instead."

"No, please, I mean, let me...oh God, who are you? What are you?"

"Questions you should have asked before you tied me up and scooped out my eyes, Mr. Optic. Too late now."

I had the spoon in my pocket, the one he used.

His screams were satisfying.

His eyes fit my sockets.

I stood back and watched the blood pouring down his face, just as it had mine, a few hours earlier. The difference was, I knew he would die.

I was about to walk out on him and his darkness forever, but paused to enjoy the moment a little longer.

"Thank you, Mr Optic. Now I can see you. I quite like what I see, too. That was for me and all the other women you mutilated and left to die. This should be a reminder to all you men who like to play murderous games... don't mess with a zombie."

272

Halloween Dream

Richard Laymon

The mist swirled and moved around Dane as he huddled in the dark alleyway. It looked like ghosts, many ghosts, all crowded together, peering over each others' shoulders in an effort to look at the runaway, to laugh, to point fingers and defy him to cry. He cowered back against the wall, determined to be strong, not to let the ghosts intimidate him. The setting sun sent red light through the thickening mist, giving them the appearance of spooks drenched in blood. Freaky weather, he told himself, low lying mist, clear skies above, sun going down, explain it away rationally and it is not blood soaked spooks but nature at her freakiest.

It didn't help.

Dane was too young and too scared to accept any rationalisation of the phenomena; he left the alleyway and ran.

He saw without really seeing the Halloween displays in the shop windows as he passed them, pumpkins whose carved faces were far from benign, witches who snarled rather than smiled, skeletons which rattled their bones at him, white sheeted spooks which leered at him with open mouths and greedy eyes.

The mist ghosts pursued him too, laughing silently at his terror, until he hid behind a Dumpster in another alley and they stopped at the entrance, seemingly bewildered and unable to see him. It was his turn to laugh, silently. Even ghosts could be outwitted, it seemed.

When it was coming up to Halloween, it was not good to be on the streets without protection. Oh yes, the monsters were supposed to wait until the 31st, but what if they didn't, what if they thought it would be fun to creep up on people who didn't have the sense to put the barriers in place... He knew all about the things he should have; garlic, a crucifix, holy water, all of it was as remote from him as the Statue of Liberty herself – and the chance to go and visit it. No money, no shelter, no food, just another runaway on the streets, alone, scared and starving. Not in any particular order, he thought, amused at his ramblings.

'Hey, kid!'

Startled, he spun round, staring into the darkness, trying to see who had called him. A shadow moved, became larger, moved toward Dane who was absolutely petrified. The fear was so intense he felt sick.

'Hey kid!' The shadow became a derelict, seemingly hanging in rags and dirt, half a loaf in one hand and a bottle in the other. The shabby coat he was wearing hung open, showing clothes tied up with string. 'Sorry, didn't mean to scare you. You on the run or something? Only you looked right scared when you came in - oh, this is my home, by the way.'

'Oh, really sorry.' Dane spluttered his words, trying to still his heart, trying to quieten the blood racing round his body. 'I didn't know.'

'Of course you didn't. How could you know? No signs are there to say this be my place.'

'I was... running from a cop.' It wouldn't do to tell the truth, that he had actually been running from the mist. It wouldn't go down very well. He was supposed to be streetwise; after all he had been out on his own now for all of two weeks – and a bit.

Trouble was he wasn't much good at it. How long did it take to become knowledgeable in the ways of the street? Obviously longer than that, or he would not be without shelter, food and friends.

'Ah, cops. They look for young meat, so they do. Pack them off to some social officer or other and tick off another success in their quota of people they've rescued. I take it you was thieving food or something, then?'

'Sort of.'

'No need to tell me, young 'un. Been where you are a thousand times. Come with me.'

Dane had nothing to lose but his life and he felt that was not worth hanging on to these days. He followed the derelict further down the alleyway, stumbling over things which squelched as he stepped on them, touched things which were slimy and repellent when he almost lost his balance so that by the time they reached the sealed off end, he was feeling sicker than ever. Should he ask what was carpeting the alleyway? No, safer to leave it to his imagination. He had the feeling that what he would be told was worse than anything he could conjure up himself.

A Dumpster had been commandeered by the derelict and used as a wall. Its wheels had vanished; it sat on the ground, sturdy, solid and safe. Behind it was a lantern, flickering its warmth against the dirty walls, revealing cardboard boxes, a stained mattress, blankets, even a small stove.

'Here.' The man pushed a blanket at Dane and pointed at the mattress. 'Sit you down there, wrap that round you. Gets a bit cold in here come night, especially when there's mist like tonight. Now, what's your name?'

As he spoke he tinkered with the stove and the good sound of something bubbling became a melodic background to his voice, which was gravel sharp but not unkind.

'Dane.'

'How long you been homeless, Dane?'

'Two weeks.'

'No chance of going back?'

'None.' Dane surprised himself with the vehemence of his reply. The derelict smiled, revealing broken blackened teeth that made him look fearsome.

'Like that, is it? Right, I'm Jonah. Not my real name, you know, something the others been calling me for years, so it's good enough for everyone. Dane. Good solid name, that, bet you come from a good solid family who don't appreciate or understand the needs of a growing boy. Right?'

Dane sat staring at the grimy wall, seeing not the discoloured bricks but his family as he had last seen them... his mother decapitated by the blast of a shotgun, his father with a knife in his neck, spouting blood like a fountain, his older sister screaming her rage and kicking wildly as the intruders tied her and carried her out the door. If he hadn't been under the stairs at the time the men broke in, he would have been dead or carried away too. It was no consolation. The images would not go.

It was my fault. All of it. Shouldn't have happened like that, they were supposed to...

In that moment the sheer desolation of his plight swept over him and he folded up, sobbing helplessly. Jonah reached out a rough hand and pulled Dane close to him. The boy was grateful for the human touch, the first he had known since that terrible time.

'Is it that bad, kid?' Jonah asked in a quiet, serious voice. Dane nodded. Sniffing and trying hard to stem the tears, he muttered into the dirty coat: 'Men broke in our house. Shot my Mam, big gun, shotgun, shot her head clean off. One threw a knife, got my Dad in the throat. My sis, Deanna, carried out she was, carried out screaming and yelling and I don't know where they took her. Took the money, took the TV and the stereo and all the nice things we had."

It tumbled out, a mass of words, bringing visions of horror beyond belief for a boy, the amount of blood, the mess his mother's head made on the carpet, the screams of his sister still echoing in his ears.

'And you were hiding, were you? Gone to get something when they came in and they didn't know you was there. Then you ran. Sensible kid you are, Dane, sensible. Down to your bones.' Dane felt an arm go round his shoulders and he snuggled closer to his rescuer. 'And you been on the streets ever since. Too scared to go home. Right?'

Dane nodded. He thought of his home, his aunts and uncles, his grandparents who would by now be

277

involved in arranging funerals while waiting for news of Deanna, if there was any, and of him, for they would think he too had been abducted. He longed for the comfort of the familiar faces, for his clothes, books, toys, his school friends, all of it left behind, hiding behind the mask of blood and brains that came between him and everything he had left.

'I can't go home,' he whispered.

I can't go home 'cos they know who I am and I know who they are and – oh God, they know, they know, but no one else does, the bullying, the torture, the pain, the need to stop them hurting me all the time. Them, Josh and Ned, had their eyes on Deanna for an age, wanting her, she didn't want them, called them scum and dirtbags and everything and everything they did made it worse for them and worse for me.

Jonah nodded, his wiry beard brushing the top of Dane's head as he did so. 'Course not. Too much blood, too many memories, too scared they might realise you saw them. Course not. You'll be all right with me, little 'un. Now, hungry, are you?'

***

After three days of living with Jonah, Dane began to accept his new life with some level of enthusiasm. Without actually saying anything, Jonah showed him where to find cast away food, bought and not eaten most of the time, half empty cans of coke and other drinks in rubbish bins, rescued a thick sweater from a dump which kept him warm without getting in the way of his sliding the occasional packet of biscuits or candy into a

278

pocket as he passed by the display. Calm, Jonah showed him, calm, no rushing away to draw attention to yourself. Walk as if you had every right to be there. He even managed to ignore the slipperiness underfoot in the alleyway and the strange sensation when he touched the walls, putting it down to damp and decay. It was a good enough explanation without asking questions and not liking the answers.

All was good and Dane was content until he brought home a newspaper for Jonah and saw his face staring out from the front page. Beside his photo was one of Deanna, which brought tears to his eyes. He threw the paper down and stood staring at Jonah.

'Now I can't go out.'

'Oh yes you can, boy, yes you can. Wait for tonight. 'Tis a full moon, if I reckon it right and we can do something which will let you go out. If you're up for it, of course.'

'Depends on what it is.'

But the boy in Dane was intrigued, even as the more mature person street life was creating thought the words were nonsensical. He was himself, how could he be any different?

'Wait and see and I'll tell you nearer the time. Don't want you worrying yourself for nothing, do we?'

'Suppose not. I suppose I get to stay here until then.'

'Right on. You rest up, tis my turn to go get the food in. I wouldn't mind a beer, too.'

Jonah shambled his way out of the alley, leaving Dane in the darkness with his thoughts. What did

Jonah have in mind? How could he be changed? Then the doubts set in; should he give himself up to the police, put the family's mind at rest that at least one of the children had survived? No, that was out of the question. Deanna was no doubt dead by now, she wouldn't be allowed to live; she had seen everything. If he went to the police, his picture would be everywhere and they would find him. Definitely they would find him. He did not want to die. He had a lot to do.

They made it clear, over and over, those two and the hangers-on they attracted, made it clear they were prepared to kill if they had to. And I believed them. Why not? They thieved and mugged and tortured and never once did the cynical smiles leave their faces. Never once.

He sat still, listening to the road noise, sirens, engines, horns, the crump of metal as car hit car, then the other sounds filtered in, a plane screaming its way into the airport, the rhythmic thump of a helicopter circling the area – traffic reports, I bet, thought Dane – voices, laughter, shouts, cries. It seemed as if the more he lived on the streets the clearer everything became, he had never been so aware of how much noise there was in a city. Or how much there was to fear. Any of those noises could mean danger for him, any of them could mean one of the two had found out where he was and made up his mind to come and get him...

He heard shuffling and tensed, his stomach contracting in sick fear, but Jonah's gravel voice assured him all was well.

'Got us some good food here, boy, got me some good beer, too. Oh, got a Coke for you, a new one. Here, enjoy!'

'I'm glad you're back!' Dane got up hugged his friend in a rare display of emotion. It seemed to take Jonah by surprise, for he sat down and stared at Dane for some time. Then he coughed and put both hands to his head.

'Damn me, boy, been a good many years since someone did that!'

'Sorry...'

'Don't you be sorry none! It were wonderful, that it were!'

They sat in silence for a while, lost in their thoughts, not able to share. Dane had some heavy burdens on his mind; they were not for Jonah, who had enough of his own.

'Right.' Jonah was all briskness and efficiency. 'Get this food in you, tis a bit warm still and good for you right now. Then we can talk.'

Talk. They had talked endlessly for three days and yet Jonah said they were to talk. Dane had stuck to his story and Jonah had respected that, not asking any questions, accepting what Dane told him. They had talked of his past life up to that time, of school, friends, family, Christmasses and birthdays, things he would never have dreamed of sharing with someone but it felt good, reliving those happy times felt so very good, covering up the pain and guilt that was otherwise tearing him apart. Where was Deanna now? Was she still alive and suffering in their hands? What brutal sex had she endured, for it was a given that they would have taken her, it was what they wanted and Dane knew it. It made the guilt even worse. But when all that had been told, all the good times and the bad times, everything but the truth of that day, what else was there to turn over and dissect – unless Jonah had an idea of what had really happened.

'Bit of fun, Daney boy, bit of fun. Let us in, we'll take Deanna away for a little while, you know, wind her up a bit, we won't harm her none, promise. We need to show her we're good guys at heart. She's got the wrong opinion of us, hasn't she? You know what we're like.'

Oh yes, he knew what they were like but with a knife carving a line down his chest, drawing a trickle of blood he knew would be obvious to his mother if she saw it, with Ned standing by tapping a staple gun on the table as if he was longing to use it on flesh, not on the table which was already studded with a thousand staples, what choice did he have?

Now I know how Judas felt. He got himself in a situation and he couldn't get out of it. If I'd've reported these bastards for bullying a year ago, six months ago, I wouldn't be here now, being carved with a knife and threatened with a staple gun and I wouldn't be seriously betraying my sister.

Only it wasn't like that.

Oh but it was, Dane! It was!

Betrayal. You told them when she would be home, you told them the best time to come, you opened the door to them, Dane! Opened the damned door for them, you did!

And hid when they charged in. And threw up when the shotgun went off. And ran when you saw the mess they made when they were done.

Somehow he ate the food, warm and tasty and filling, he noted. The Coke was good too, full of fizz. Everyone before this had gone flat, leaving only the taste behind and without the bubbles, it wasn't the same.

He almost felt like a human being again, not a guilt ridden wreck of a teenager who had somehow gotten on the wrong side of a gang of bullies who had terrified him. With appalling consequences.

What did Jonah have in mind?

The old man seemed to take an age to eat his food. Maybe he had bad teeth, mused Dane, ones that made it hard to eat, maybe it hurt to eat. Whatever, he wished Jonah would hurry so they could get on with the talking. He had the feeling it was big, serious and scary all at the same time. Thinking on that, did he want Jonah to stop eating and start talking?

His stomach said no. His heart said yes. Somewhere in the middle his brain decided it had no feelings one way or the other, provided he stayed safe, which was all that mattered to him.

Outside of the need for revenge, that was.

Revenge. That burning need to take the two men and their hangers'-on and torment them the way they had tormented him. To draw a long open bleeding raw line down their chests, carve their initials in the living skin, watch them writhe under the blade, watch them lose control of themselves when they realised that the victim had become the killer. For he would, he would without a second thought, kill them stone dead. And walk away and be proud of what he had done.

'Been watching your thoughts, boy.' Jonah sucked at the bottle of beer and looked at Dane. 'You show your emotions a bit easy, you know, but then you trusts old Jonah, don't you?'

Dane nodded, but said nothing.

'I saw your face; it went from fear to anger and determination. I think, tell me I'm wrong, boy, if I am, tell me I got it completely wrong but if you found those men who took your family from you, there would be killing, right?'

'Right.' Dane stared back at Jonah. 'What chance...'

'Every chance. One step at a time, boy, one step at a time. We're dealing with the full moon tonight; we gotta get past this bit first and then see where we go. Nearly Halloween, we can do things that night we can't do other nights, but first we have to make ourselves ready.'

The lantern flickered out. Dane felt a sliver of ice go through him, the darkness was all consuming, impenetrable, frightening. A hand touched his shoulder and he stifled a shriek. Jonah grunted with amusement. ''Tis only me, boy, who else did you think would be in here?'

'The lantern...'

'Ran out of fuel, is all. But as it happens, it's good. What we have to say is best said in the dark.'

The silence between them was as thick as the darkness itself. Dane felt he had to say something but couldn't find the words. If Jonah would only speak...

He did but then Dane wished he hadn't.

'So, what really happened, boy? 'Tis a lot more to that story than you be telling.'

'How ... how did you know?'

'You be too well educated, too – cared for, to be a true runaway. No one after you in the family, no parents beating you up, nothing like that. Am I right? No need to answer, I know I am. So, what happened that day?'

'I...' The words spilled suddenly, the darkness helping to hide his emotions and Jonah's.

'These guys, they were in the last year at school when I started. They picked on me from the start, don't know why, do they need a reason to bully someone? Stole my money, my books, my clothes, twisted my arm, near enough dislocated my shoulder one time when I tried to fight back. Then they took to following me everywhere. School's been a time of terror; believe me it has, never thought it would end. Some days they wouldn't be there, other days they would. Never knew what and where and why. They followed me home and they saw Deanna. You saw the picture, Jonah, she's beautiful, right?'

Jonah grunted.

'No one listened to me when I told them. Said it was all in my head and I should get on with life. Parents, teachers, friends, no one believed me 'cos no one saw them near me, they took good care of that! Then they left and I thought I was free. No. They went right on following me, taking me to their hideout, burning me with cigarettes, cutting me with their knives, because they wanted Deanna and she didn't want them.

'When it got serious, when they were threatening to kill me, I had to do what they wanted, tell them when she would be home. They said it was a joke. I

285

knew it wasn't. I went to the cops that night but they laughed at me and told me to go home. I did. Next day they burst in and shot Mum and Dad ...'

He faltered, gathered his strength and went on. 'Now I want nothing more than to find them and kill them. Slowly. The slower the better. Starve them to death. Deprive them of their reason to live. Pay them back for years of torment and what they did to my family. I will pay any price – any price at all – to do that.'

'Mercy save us, that's one hell of a story, boy. You been holding a lot in for a lot of years and it all blew up in the end. Damnation on those cops who laughed at you, I say. Right...'

The figure stirred in the darkness and Dane thought, for a moment, he saw an outline of light around Jonah. Impossible, the blackness was impenetrable. He wasn't afraid and for the first time, he felt as if he was purged of all that the hurt he had suffered all the years.

'I can help you, Dane. I can help you but there's a price.'

'What?'

'You won't be the same again when we're through.'

'Not sure what you mean.'

'Course you don't. I'm not the derelict you think I am, boy, I got powers. I been helping people best I can for a goodly number of years, that I have, with the help of a dark angel. You know what I mean, boy?'

'A demon?'

'Right first time. I wasn't sure about him and you, not till the day you give me that hug. Ain't no one done that in a mountain of years. Rare touched my heart, that did and he spoke with me that night, spoke in my head like he does, asked me to find out your story and he would see what he could do. He's right here alongside me now. He's ready to change you, Dane, change you just a little so you can do what you need to do.'

'I can't change back, is that what you're saying?'

'Right, boy. Right first time. Your choice. You get this one chance and then, who knows? You could go back to what's left of your family.'

A sudden longing swept through Dane, to be held by his loving grandmother for a moment, to see his grandfather's friendly grin and go fishing with him, to see his aunts and uncles, all would be sorrowing over the deaths and thinking he was dead, too.

'How do I go back?'

'One step at a time. Ain't I told you that already? Tonight's the full moon. Tonight you can take that first step, let the dark angel here change you. Then you get your revenge, then you see how you can go home. One step, another step, another step. Tis important, Dane, boy, tis important you know you won't be the same – after.'

'Will anyone else know I am different?'

'Nope. You thought I was just some old drunk, didn't you? You ain't thought any different all the time you've been here, right?'

'And you were changed?'

'Sure enough was. Most drunks get murdered by hoodlums and thrill seekers. Not Jonah.'

'Don't you want to go home?'

Jonah sighed and the sound was every sad thing Dane had ever heard.

'I had a wife, Dane. Right beautiful she was too; most beautiful thing ever walked this earth. Loved her beyond all sense and reason, I did. She was mugged right out there in the street, smashed her lovely face in, he did. I went to drink then and ended up here and the dark angel found me and showed me how to get my revenge. Cornered him, I did, smashed his face in, but not like he did hers, I did it slowly, bit by bit, gouged out his eyes one at a time, smashed his nose, tore off his ears, one at a time, cut his mouth until it were a huge blood ridden grin, carved initials into his cheeks and forehead. Then I killed him.'

Dane sat, mouth open, visualising the blood, the pain and the shrieking that would have gone with the killing – and knew he wanted it, wanted it so much it was a physical pain.

'And I never went home because all I had to live for was gone. I thought. Then I found out that sometimes, just sometimes, runaways like you came to find me and I could help them and it makes living just about worthwhile.'

For the second time Dane reached across and hugged his friend, ignoring the smelly coat and the unwashed smell. He didn't fare much better himself.

'I'm ready.'

The darkness alongside Jonah changed; a vivid crimson glow outlined a man, one who appeared to be a solid lump of muscle. The face was almost human, the eyes definitely were not. The glow became stronger and the man, the only way Dane could describe him, became clearer. And terrifying.

Dane felt every part that was outside his body trying to crawl into his body and hide.

'We need no lanterns.' The voice was not quite right, someone trying to be human but not quite making it. 'I make light. I make you strong. I make you fit to fight. I make you a killing machine. I give you take. You learn to control it. You agree?'

Dane thought for a moment. He was young enough to want the ability to take revenge and old enough to know he would have a hard job controlling it, but it was worth it. Oh yes, it was worth it.

'I agree.'

It was like burning coals heaped on his head and body; he almost cried out but gritted his teeth and waited as the pain swept through him.

'Hold on, boy!' Jonah was doing his best to help and his voice did give Dane the courage to hang on against all the odds, knowing that sooner or later the pain would go. It was what was giving him his new abilities, he knew that. Even as he thought it, the pain began to lessen, to creep from his feet back up his legs, through his body and finally out through his head.

'Strong person.'

'I knew it,' agreed Jonah. 'I don't give you just anyone, do I?'

'You good servant of the Dark Master.'

'And this one will be, too.'

'You are right.'

Even as he watched, the crimson glow faded and the demon, whatever it was, returned to the darkness. Dane was sure he was still there, though, watching, listening, waiting with the patience only demons can truly know. He wondered why he wasn't afraid.

'Dane, there ain't nothin' you can't do now, boy, short of flying across this city by flapping your arms. You can fight anyone and win. You can stand up to any man and know your look will bring him down, make him back off. You can find the tormentors and you can kill them, as fast or as slow as you want. Your choice. You just got a gift few get, use it well.'

Dane stood up and reached for the grimy ceiling of the alleyway. He felt as if he could punch his way through it, but didn't, his friend would lose his home if he did. He turned round and stared at Jonah.

'That – that stuff – I walked on to get in here and walked on to get out, it isn't animal, is it?'

'Nope.'

'That's what I thought. It's them who tried to mug you for your booze, right? Fools.'

Dane felt about twice his age, in thought and in body. He was ready to go out and find those who had taken his sister and his life, ready to wreak total vengeance on them but Jonah put a hand on his arm and held him back.

'This is the first step, boy, like I told you. Now, rest easy and let it build inside you. Slowly and surely, let it build. All right?'

'Makes sense, yes.'

'Reason I say it, boy, is this. Three days' time it's Halloween. You can go out there on the streets, with mask and costume and everything and go do what you wanna do without anyone seeing you.

290

Right? Then, when it's done and you're satisfied, you can take off the costume and go home.'

Home. If anything was a Halloween dream, it was that, going home, even if it was to fewer people than he had been with before. But home...

Three days.

A small amount of time to wait to pay back years of torment and loss. To take revenge and then go home with blood on his hands and peace in his heart. Could he live with that?

Jonah must have read his thoughts. 'You can live with it, Dane, my boy; you can live with it because you will have found peace, the kind that only comes when there is blood on your hands.'

Three days to his Halloween dream. Yes, he could wait. But once the magical witching date arrived he would go out into the world –

And the world had best watch out.

Nothing would ever be the same again.

The contributors to this collection...

Yul Brynner

I began editing an anthology for Static Movement, 'Ghost Stories, Western Style' which was not filling as fast as I would have liked. I thought it would be good to write something myself to add to the book and sent out a thought, would someone like to write a Western story with me. Yul Brynner arrived in full Westworld outfit... grinning that evil grin that he seemed to wear throughout the film. The story is utterly surreal and fits perfectly into that anthology. It does pretty well here, too...

Roald Dahl

Surely one of the greatest names in short story writing, Roald Dahl came as a welcome presence to give me some of the more subtle and intriguing stories in this collection. He is always welcome, he knows that. He comes with smiles and a sense of mystery at times, this man has never revealed all of himself and I doubt he ever will.

Virgil 'Gus' Grissom

It isn't every day a famous astronaut walks into my office and asks if he can write a story. At that time I was looking for stories to send to an anthology entitled "Frozen Fear Deluxe' for Static Movement. 'I have a story for you,' he said... and he had, too. Virgil has not been to see me since that time, but the memory of his visit lingers still, powerful presence and overwhelmingly friendly man. He is overawed and pleased with the ongoing remembrance of him.

Kathryn Howard

Buckingham's story was intended for an anthology entitled 'Beyond The Grave', restless spirits with unfinished business. Kathryn Howard came with a story for the same anthology and incidentally, to settle her mind, too, about her love for Thomas Culpepper. I was delighted to work with her, even after I found myself unable to sleep and busy writing with her at 2 AM...

Richard Laymon

I have been a horror fan for many years; it has influenced my writing quite considerably over time. When I became aware that Richard Laymon was in my life I was extremely pleased. He told me that he might be 'dead' but that he had many more horror stories to tell. We began a YA novel, which we are still working on, to offset the historical work I was – and am – doing in between all this other work. Richard (known to me as Rich, as I have several other Richard's in my life) is a larger than life presence. His stories range from relatively normal to outright gore, depending on his mood at the time. They always capture my imagination from the outset and never let go.

Bela Lugosi

293

I was reading a posting about a new vampire themed anthology, saying to Rich 'shame I don't do vampire stuff.' Within minutes I was writing a vampire story, which was not Rich's style or theme. I asked who was writing with me, and got back 'Bela.' This delightful, charismatic film star turns out to be a fine writer as well, with some offbeat ideas. He tells me there are more stories to come. The use of butter to seal a place, mentioned in 'Keeping The Ghosts Away' he tells me is a piece of ancient folklore passed on to him by his grandmother. I am not entirely sure he is being serious, but that's what I was told. Who am I to argue with Bela Lugosi?

Richard Neville, Earl of Warwick

This is another name you would not expect to find in a collection of dark tales, but Warwick is a force to be reckoned with at the best of times. His men are part of the protection which I need whilst working with spirit and Warwick himself has visited quite a few times. He really wanted to tell this story. I am very pleased he did.

George Villiers, duke of Buckingham

Buckingham is not the 'usual' author you would expect to find in a collection of horror stories, but I had already been working with his Grace so I was not entirely surprised when he came in, flamboyant and outrageous as ever, to ask if he could write a story for the book. He and I had been working on his section of my book 'Fools And Kings And Fighting Men', the life of Charles I. I knew then that he was a talented writer, this story proves it.

Edith Wharton

I wrote 'Autumn Leaves' a long time before any of these other stories appeared and wondered who had written it with me. It is a surprisingly delicate story, revealing a deep insight into the human condition, as well as being a lovely ghost story. I realised that some of my other stories were also delicate and so I asked who was writing them with me. The name Edith Wharton was given along with a big smile and a sense of gratitude for being recognised. Several of the stories in this collection are from this talented lady. I hope for a lot more in the future.

Antony Woodville

Constant companion and resident clown, Antony Woodville also happens to be the author of the very first book published in England by William Caxton. If anyone has a right to be included, he does! He is a fine writer, as his two stories in this collection prove. Both are based on fact, with the embellishment only a good writer can bring to such stories.

CREDITS

Autumn Leaves

Published in *Something Dark In The Doorway* edited by Gregory Miller, Static Movement 2010

Back Where I Belong

Published in *Pot Luck* edited by Chris Bartholomew, Static Movement, 2011

Beaters

Published in *Changelings*, edited by George Wilhite, Static Movement, 2011

Beauty Sleeps

Published in *Ruby Red Cravings*, edited by Brianna Stoddard, Static Movement, 2011

Blood On The Rose

Published in *Beyond The Grave*, edited by Shane Collins, Static Movement, 2011

Burning Love

Published in *Twisted Love* edited by Chris Bartholomew, Static Movement, 2011

Crossroads Blues

Published in *Oil* edited by Martin Zeigler, Static Movement, 2011

The Day Death Wore Boots

Published in *Ghost Stories, Western Style* edited by Dorothy Davies, Static Movement, 2011

Do You Happen To Have...

Published in *Shadows Within Shadows*, edited by Gregory Miller, Static Movement, 2011

For The Greater Good

Published in *Dark Deeds In History* edited by Dorothy Davies, Static Movement 2011

The Fragrance Of A Poisoned Flower

Published in *Beyond The Grave* edited by Shane Collins, Static Movement 2011

Gabriel's Revenge

Published in *Reign In Heaven, Serve In Hell* edited by Naomi Jay, Static Movement, 2011

Halloween Dream

Published in *Halloween Frights II*, edited by Chris Bartholomew, Static Movement, 2011

I Bid You Welcome...

Published in *Ruby Red Cravings*, edited by Brianna Stoddard, Static Movement, 2011

I Will Wait For You

Published in *Weird City* edited by George Wilhite, Static Movement, 2011

Just A Small Thing

Published in *Sowing The Seeds of Horror* edited by Lorraine Horrell, Static Movement, 2011

Letters I've Written

Published in *Short Sips of Coffee*, Wicked East Press, 2011

Life Changes

Published in *One Hour* edited by Dorothy Davies, Static Movement, 2011

Keeping The Ghosts Away

Published in *Shadows Within Shadows*, edited by Gregory Miller, Static Movement, 2011

The Kingmaker Is Dead, Long Live The King

Published in *Dark Dispatches* edited by George Wilhite, Static Movement, 2011 **Mother Misery**

Published in *Best Left Buried* edited by Gregory Miller, Static Movement, 2011

Night Feeds

Published in *Sleepwalkin' and Picklockin'* edited by Chris Bartholomew, Static Movement, 2011

No Witnesses

Published in *Closet Monsters*, edited by Chris Bartholomew, Static Movement, 2011

The Perfect Crime

Published in *Weird City II* edited by George Wilhite, Static Movement, 2011

The Pied Piper's Story

Published in *Grim Fairy Tales* edited by Dorothy Davies, Static Movement 2011

Road Rage

Published in *Road Trip* edited by Chris Bartholomew, Static Movement, 2011

Santa's Special

Published in *Daily Flash 2012: 366 Days Of Flash Fiction*, Pill Hill Press, 2012

The Tourist

Published in *Weird City 3 edited by George Wilhite,* Static Movement, 2012

Towton Nightmare

Published in *Tales of the Sword,* edited by Dorothy Davies, Red Skies Publishing, 2012

Transformation

Published in *Ruby Red Cravings* edited by Brianna Stoddard, Static Movement, 2011

Waiting for the 9.03

Published in *Midnight Train,* edited by Dorothy Davies, Static Movement 2011

When Wightlink Became Darklink

Published in *The Shadow People* edited by Chris Bartholomew, Static Movement, 2011